THE GREAT HUNGER

Paul G. Andrews, Thomas Keneally,
Meg Keneally and Roland Joffé

dizzyemupublishing.com

DIZZY EMU PUBLISHING
1714 N McCadden Place, Hollywood, Los Angeles 90028
www.dizzyemupublishing.com

THE GREAT HUNGER
Paul G. Andrews, Thomas Keneally, Meg Keneally and Roland Joffé

First published in the United States
in 2021 by Dizzy Emu Publishing

Copyright © 2021 by Paul G. Andrews, Thomas Keneally, Meg Keneally and Roland Joffé

Paul G. Andrews, Thomas Keneally, Meg Keneally
and Roland Joffé have asserted their rights under
the Copyright, Designs and Patents Act 1988 to be
identified as the authors of this work.

1 3 5 7 9 10 8 6 4 2

This book is sold subject to the condition that it
shall not, by way of trade or otherwise, be lent,
resold, hired out, or otherwise circulated without the
publisher's prior consent in any form of binding or
cover other than that in which it is published and
without a similar condition, including this condition,
being imposed on the subsequent purchaser.

dizzyemupublishing.com

THE GREAT HUNGER

Paul G. Andrews, Thomas Keneally,
Meg Keneally and Roland Joffé

<u>THE GREAT HUNGER</u>

FINAL DRAFT

Written by

Paul G Andrews
Tom Keneally
Meg Keneally
Roland Joffé

Paul G Andrews, Producer
GlobalWatch Films
602 Falcon Wharf
London, SW11 3RF
44(0)203 086 9616

WGA REGISTERED NOV 2020

EXT. SEA WATERFORD. IRELAND 1847 - DAWN

HAUNTING MUSIC - Harp, Voice and Pipe.

WIDE ANGLE: Dawn sun tips the foaming tops of the dark WAVES.

>   ANNE(V.O.)
>   In the bleakest and most barren of
>   landscapes a flower will find a
>   foothold and bloom. So it is with
>   love, that may blossom, thank God,
>   even on the edge of hell itself

A CART drawn by two THIN HORSES creaks its way along the beach. Whatever it contains is covered with a tattered grey TARPAULIN.

Two skinny, weary MALE FIGURES precede the cart along the shoreline. They see something and call out to the driver of the cart, which comes to a halt as the men walk into the waves.

ANGLE: SHORELINE.

>   ANNE (V.O.)
>   In 1845 the potato blight crossed
>   the ocean from America and reached
>   the shores of Ireland, destroying
>   the harvest.

A skeletal HAND, seems to beckon us, the waves roll a half naked and starved body towards us. A GIRL, maybe only ten. Her mouth stained green, her eyes sightless.

ANGLE: CART. The DRIVER throws back the tarpaulin. A glimpse of its content: layers of the dead.

Silently the men load the dead girl into the cart.

>   ANNE (V.O.)
>   As the blight spread across Ireland
>   well over a million people
>   succumbed to death through
>   starvation and illness.

EXT. GALWAY. BURIAL GROUND. CLIFDEN WORKHOUSE - DAY

ROW upon ROW of cheap deal COFFINS stretch before us. The CART from the beach unloads its sad cargo. The dead girl is placed in a COFFIN, head to foot with another DEAD CHILD.

ANGLE: the cart leaves, empty now and ready to be refilled.

EXT. GALWAY. CLIFDEN WORKHOUSE. GATES - DAY

A CROWD of the destitute, emaciated and starving, surround the WORKHOUSE gates, which are being opened for the morning admissions. A sign above the gates reads.

"For the encouragement of Industry and the Relief of Want"

The cart exits the gates, passing the despairing crowd. A WOMAN sits on the ground nursing a dying child.

ANGLE: A smartly turned out PHAETON carriage passes the workhouse. The two occupants (who we come to meet later) stare nonchalantly out at the desperate crowd.

INT. GALWAY. CLIFDEN WORKOUSE. PHAETON - CONTINIOUS.

The younger of two men, THOMAS FRANCIS MEAGHER, 24, tall and handsome, slightly dandified, sighs and glances down at the NEWSPAPER lying on his lap. It is called the NATION and it's headline reads "Call for an armed uprising against English rule".

The OLDER MAN, THOMAS MEAGHER, 56, leans forward and taking the paper off his son's lap crumples it up and tosses it out of the window.

Father and son stare at each other, but nothing is said.

> ANNE (V.O.)
> Now the only hope for those parts
> of the country not yet affected was
> the potato harvest of 1847.

EXT. TIPPERARY CAHIR MANOR AND FIELDS - MORNING

A fog moves over rows of potato plants, working its way up to a grand manor on the hill overlooking the fields.

The camera pans down the hill, over the fog laden fields, to find Cahir village below. A large BUILDING with the word GRANARY incised on it is guarded by two RED COATED SOLDIERS.

EXT. CAHIR POTATO FIELDS - MORNING

GRACE DELOREY, beautiful, intelligent and headstrong, early 20s, sings a hopeful Irish harvest hymn as she walks through the fog toward the fields. She's flanked by her half sister, CLODAGH, 13, and her strong matriarch, ANNE DELOREY, 43, mixed race, a kind Mother but strong willed and resilient, (she's had to be) who is our narrator.

All three woman carry empty baskets, and nervously look out towards the MEN with loys (Irish spades), who advance towards the rows of potato plants around the little village.

TIM Delorey, 55, tall, respected in the community, powerful looking but kind, very short sighted and real family man, Grace's father, and her half brother NEALL, 12, brave beyond his years, reach their rows. Tim takes an anxious breath as he leans to examine a potato plant.

To Tim's horror, its leaves are covered in brown blotches.

Tim shows the plant to Neall, who reels back in shock. Neall runs from plant to plant, checking leaf after leaf. Every single one is covered in dark spots and blotches.

Tim begins frantically to dig, Neall alongside him. Tim throws his loy aside and kneels, scrabbling in the dirt.

His hands uncover a small part of a potato. He crosses himself, and extracts it. But the potato dissolves into a black, oozing mess.

He stands, flings the potato aside and tries another row, digging up potatoes, and flinging them aside when they all prove to be putrid. Neall does the same.

Finally, they reach the last row. Tim begins to dig, slowly this time, as Neall stands silent witness. Tim brings up a potato and shows his son. It looks unblighted, and Neall begins to laugh.

Then, before their eyes, a dark blotch appears on the skin of the potato and begins to spread.

Tim crushes the potato in his hand, and black rot oozes between his fingers. He drops to his knees and begins to sob, as Neall looks on, horrified.

Grace, Anne, and Clodagh arrive at the family plot.

Grace abruptly stops singing when she sees her father. Anne drops her basket and runs to Tim, as Grace and Clodagh follow. Grace stares as her parents kneel in the dirt, her mother holding her father as he sobs.

The sound of a wicked wind rises.

INT. CAHIR VILLAGE. DELOREY COTTAGE SMALL UPPER ROOM - DAY

The wind blasts the humble cottage.

CU: Grace peers at her face in a PIECE OF MIRROR.

                    CLODAGH (O.S.)
          I'm bleeding out the back Ma.

                    ANNE (O.S.)
          You didn't let her eat the
          rotten...

                    TIM (O.S.)
          She snuck back and dug 'em up
          herself.

                    CLODAGH (O.S.)
          I thought... They might still fill
          a belly, even stinking as they are.

Sighing, Grace makes a decision. She smooths her hair. She crosses to the straw bed and hastily tucks the PAMPHLET lying on it under the thin coverlet - not before we have seen it's title "THE NATION."

                    ANNE (V.O.)
          They are poison now, my love.

INT. CAHIR. DELOREY COTTAGE. LOWER ROOM - CONTINUOUS.

Tim is huddled by the fire, Anne sits with Clodagh.

                    TIM
          We have no choice, now. There's the
          pig we've been keeping.

                    ANNE
          And the bed linens. Which will need
          washing now that...

Anne motions in the direction of Clodagh. Grace appears from upstairs.

                    GRACE
          I'm going up to the Manor. Walsh
          has put it about that Lady Mangan
          wants a new housemaid.

Anne and Tim exchange looks.

                    GRACE (CONT'D)
          Beggars can't be choosers, Mam

Before Anne can answer there is a knock at the door. Grace answers it to admit FATHER CLEARY, 60s, the approachable, plump, ever anxious parish priest.

FATHER CLEARY
Terrible news! None of the fields are free of it, I'm hearing.

GRACE
I'd best be going. Doubtless I won't be the only one applying. I hear Lady Mangan has an eye for detail.

With a smile she leaves. Fondly they watch her go. Anne tuts.

ANNE
She'll be needing to pull her neck in a little, if she's to work at the big house.

FATHER CLEARY
In truth it's about Grace that I have come here. Word is she has been somewhat outspoken. In her opinions. Rather too critical, if I may say so.

ANNE
My daughter is no church mouse, if that's what you mean father. She has been encouraged to have a mind of her own...

Father Cleary chuckles.

FATHER CLEARY
Indeed. No church mouse. Indeed not!

EXT. CAHIR. DILLON'S COTTAGE - DAY

DILLON CULHANE (23), intense, handsome face, thin but with a lean strength is tying a PIG to the back of a SMALL HANDCART that is loaded with small HOUSEHOLD items

A BURLY LABOURER, PATRICK POWER(45), appears at his elbow.

PATRICK
You're never selling that pig too, are you Dillon? I were you I'd keep the beast and feed off it for the winter.

DILLON
Because I can make the pennies it'll bring last longer than the pig itself.

Patrick nods wearily.

                    PATRICK
          Least they're paying me to build
          that damn government road to
          nowhere...

Dillon has noticed something at the end of the street. Patrick follows his gaze.

POV. Grace making her way past the Granary It is guarded by FOUR BRITISH SOLDIERS in their RED UNIFORMS, who eye her appreciatively.

Dillon feeling the accustomed pang of anxiety that Grace unconsciously unleashes in him, bends down and fiddles with the pig's rope. Patrick laughs.

                    PATRICK (CONT'D)
          Everyone knows you'se soft on
          Grace, man. Why don't you tell her?

                    DILLON
          Will you hold your peace now,
          Patrick!

Patrick chuckles. He hefts his STONE BREAKER'S MALLET.

                    PATRICK
          Well, I'm off. It's the road or the
          workhouse.

Dillon nods a goodbye. He looks up when he hears Grace's voice.

                    GRACE (OS)
          Good morning, Dillon.

She smiles.

                    DILLON
          Good morning, Grace. Not that
          there's much good about it...

He stops unhappy with that gambit. Not sure what to say next.

                    GRACE
          Terrible times, Dillon

                    DILLON
          Fate's dealt us a terrible blow.
          That's certain.

GRACE
Fate is it Dillon? The Nation says it's a deliberate policy.

DILLON
Is that what they say?

GRACE
By our masters in London to subjugate the people of Ireland.

DILLON
They'll have to watch what they print or they'll be closed down...

GRACE
According to Father Cleary, and the other wise men of the parish, doubtless.

DILLON
Let's not start that again, Grace. Eh?

He looks the rope clasped in his rough hands.

DILLON (CONT'D)
Well...

Grace waits, staring at him disconcertingly. A beat:

DILLON (CONT'D)
Best be getting to market.

She nods, disappointed in spite of herself. She turns to go.

DILLON (CONT'D)
So you'll be on your way to church yourself then?

GRACE
Church?

DILLON
All dandied up like you's going to a christening.

He says, teasingly. She replies in kind.

GRACE
And what's it to you? Dillon Culhane?

                    DILLON
          Must have spent all morning in
          front of that mirror of yours!

Meant as a compliment, but she bridles.

                    GRACE
          I'm going up to the Manor, it is,
          Dillon.

                    DILLON
          Well, pardon me if I don't keep you
          from your visit, Grace. The Manor
          of course... Like I said, I've to
          get to market.

He turns away.

                    GRACE
          There's a position open...

But he is already pushing the cart away and does not hear
her. She rolls her eyes and heads off.

Dillon glances back over his shoulder and watches Grace's
retreating back. He sighs in frustration at himself, then
walks on.

EXT. DOCKS. WATERFORD. WATERFORD COUNTY - DAY

Bustle, The UNION JACK flies on SHIPS LOADING GRAIN, FIRKINS
OF BUTTER and SLABS OF SALT BEEF. A sight observed by a small
group of GENTLEMAN MERCHANTS. One, a PIMPLY, overdressed
YOUTH turns to his dashing companion THOMAS FRANCIS MEAGHER.

                    PIMPLES
          Does it not trouble your conscience
          Thomas? All that food shipped to
          England and the blight starving
          half of Ireland?

An OLDER MERCHANT butts in sarcastically.

                    OLDER MERCHANT
          Conscience be damned, Martin. It's
          a magnificent autumn morning, the
          Sun is shining and you've full use
          of your testicles. Life is good.
          Eh, Thomas?

                    MEAGHER
          It is indeed, and that's why.

What they are staring at now is a superb WHITE MARE, that is being unloaded in SLING from one of the ships.

                    PIMPLES
          Set you back five hundred Guineas
          you say?

His companion answers without taking his eyes off the struggling horse. Meagher, is already making a name for himself as a man of substance. He grins ruefully.

                    MEAGHER
          Five hundred I don't have. Yet!

As the Mare, spooked, lands on the dock he steps forward and in spite of the warnings from his companions walks fearlessly up to the rearing animal.

He ducks under the mare's flying hoofs.

                    MEAGHER (CONT'D)
          Calm down my beauty. I know you
          have mettle, that's why I chose
          you!

He extends a hand, holding a small LUMP OF SUGAR. The horse calms but stands breathing heavily and moving skittishly as it looks at Meagher. It ignores the sugar.

Meagher chuckles, turns to his anxious companions.

                    MEAGHER (CONT'D)
          A rare filly. Can't be bribed.

He turns back to the mare. Her sides heave and she snorts but otherwise remains still.

                    MEAGHER (CONT'D)
          Can you my darling?

He steps closer to the animal, which shivers but does not flinch. Meagher reaches for the bridle. The mare snorts. Meagher steps closer. He speaks softly, not challenging.

                    MEAGHER (CONT'D)
          It's words that'll get to you isn't
          it my beauty? The music of words,
          hmm? Loving words and praise.
          That's what'll calm you. That's
          what'll win you. Is that not it?

And indeed the Mare calms, allowing Meagher to come close. His face rests against the horse's cheek. He glances at his companions.

                    MEAGHER (CONT'D)
          There now. I shall name her Juno.
          Chief goddess of the Romans
          Because she is a force of nature.
                    (To the mare)
          As indeed you are, my darling. A
          force of nature.

After a beat the horse rests her head on his shoulder.

EXT. CAHIR HOUSE. TIPPERARY - DAY

The sun is higher in the sky. CAHIR HOUSE, grand home to Lady Mangan, stands in idyllic grounds. The stable and byres are peaceful on this autumn afternoon. Except for the small desperate FAMILY that has clustered near the gates that lead to the Manor House.

Walsh a stocky, hard headed, Yorkshire man, hurries from the house towards them making shooing gestures as one might to a flock of geese. FERGAL SHANAHAN (late 20s), lean, tough as nails, respectful but firm, stands his ground.

                    WALSH
          Be off with you, Shanahan! There's
          a set time for your business here,
          and this is not it.

                    FERGAL
          I have come to speak to her
          ladyship, Walsh, face to face.

                    WALSH
          Mister Walsh to you, Shanahan, and
          any talking you'll do with me.
          Should I choose to listen.

                    FERGAL
          Fat chance. It was *your* cronies
          came this morning with orders to
          throw us out of our home...

Walsh cuts him off.

                    WALSH
          They came to collect rents overdue,
          Shanahan and they gave you five
          days to pay!

INT. CAHIR HOUSE. ANTE ROOM. - CONTINUOUS

Grace sits uncomfortably on a stiff backed and somewhat worn Jacobean Chair. Fergal's voice floats through the open casement. Grace gets up and peers out of the window.

POV: Fergal tries to push past Walsh.

                        FERGAL
              Lady Mangan! Lady Mangan! I'll not
              leave here till I have spoken with
              you!

Walsh calls to a BURLY red coated SERGEANT who has appeared from the farm house.

                        WALSH
              Sergeant!

Grace watches sadly, pained by this all too familiar scene. A voice startles her.

                        MRS WALSH
              Her Ladyship will see you now,
              Delorey.

Mrs WALSH is tiny and known as "Parrot" by the Cahir staff because of her habit of repeating her husbands orders. With a last glance out of the window, Grace follows her.

INT. CAHIR HOUSE. LADY MANGAN'S BED CHAMBER - DAY

The DRAPES are half closed and the room is gloomy. Lady Serena Mangan, attractive, self centered, early 40s, foreign widower and second wife of the recently deceased Lord Mangan, sits in an overstuffed WING CHAIR, eyes shaded by a white hand against what little light there is. A small PEKINESE (Sinbad) lies asleep in a basket at her feet.

                        MRS WALSH
              Your Ladyship. Grace Delorey. As
              you requested.

Faintly, from outside, Fergal calls out for Lady Mangan. After a pause her Ladyship lifts her hand and looks at Grace, waiting by the door..

                        LADY MANGAN
              You should know I am prone to
              migraines, umm...

                        MRS WALSH
              Grace, your ladyship.

                        LADY MANGAN
              I know the girl's name, Walsh. I am
              distracted by that commotion
              outside.
                             (MORE)

                        LADY MANGAN (CONT'D)
                I'd have thought Mister Walsh would
                have made certain I was protected
                against that kind of thing!

This is too much for Grace.

                        GRACE
                Best protection against "that kind
                of thing" would be to halt all
                evictions..!

A beat. Mrs Walsh sucks in her breath.

                        MRS WALSH
                Mind your tongue, girl!

Lady Mangan silences her with a wave.

                        LADY MANGAN
                Hold your peace, Walsh. The girl is
                inclined to speak and I am inclined
                to listen.

Walsh sniffs. Lady Mangan gestures at Grace and says softly.

                        LADY MANGAN (CONT'D)
                You were about to say?

She leans forwards into the light. She looks unworldly pale.

A beat: Grace looks sidelong at Mrs Walsh:

                        GRACE
                Evicting a family that is unable to
                pay its rent is to ruin them beyond
                redemption. Especially now. To
                condemn them to the work house and
                separation. It is inhumane and
                unworthy.

She stops. Lady Mangan nods at her sympathetically.

                        LADY MANGAN
                Unworthy?

Grace goes for it.

                        GRACE
                Unworthy of someone who calls
                themselves a Christian and...

                        LADY MANGAN
                And?

                    GRACE
          Those that have, should not
          disregard their responsibility to
          those that have not. As the good
          Lord taught us.

Lady Mangan shields her eyes again behind her deathly white
hand. She appears to be thinking. Then she says:

                    LADY MANGAN
          Very prettily said. Thank you.

A beat. Grace wonders whether to continue. Mrs Walsh can
barely contain her fury.

                    LADY MANGAN (CONT'D)
          I am getting a headache. Excuse me.
          The interview is over.

She waves the women away. A beat. Grace follows Walsh out.

When they have gone Lady Mangan leans forward and picks the
little PEKINESE out of its basket.

                    LADY MANGAN (CONT'D)
          She sounds just like my late
          husband, don't you think, Sinbad?
          And he, poor thing, died bankrupt,
          you are going to say, aren't you?

She kisses the little dog.

                    LADY MANGAN (CONT'D)
          But don't worry, little one, that
          is NOT a fate I will allow to
          happen to us. Not while I have
          brain or breath. No, no, no!

EXT. GRANARY. CAHIR - DAY

Lt ARTHUR SINCLAIR, 26, and FOUR CAVALRYMAN (REDCOATS) are
saddling up. He glances up to see an elegant figure of Thomas
Francis Meagher on his WHITE MARE trotting up the sloping
road. Behind the rider, Patrick, other LABORERS and a ROAD
FOREMAN mill about in angry discussion.

Meagher rides up to Sinclair.

                    MEAGHER
          Can you direct me to Cahir House?

                    SINCLAIR
          Indeed I can, Sir. And if you
          permit, I'll ride there with you
          myself. The village is in a restive
          state today.

Meagher follows Sinclair's look at the arguing men.

                    MEAGHER
          So I see. Not for the first time I
          imagine.

Sinclair chuckles wryly as he mounts up.

                    SINCLAIR
          Nor the last, I'll wager.

EXT. CAHIR. LOWER ROAD TO CAHIR HOUSE - DAY

WS: Stunning countryside. Meagher and Sinclair ride towards the Manor house.

                    SINCLAIR
          What brings you to Cahir, Sir?

                    MEAGHER
          Grain. My father has a bid in for
          the Mangan harvest.

                    SINCLAIR
          That won't make you very popular in
          these parts. Villagers have been
          eyeing that grain for weeks.

His evident scorn makes it an uncomfortable moment. Both men assessing the other.

                    MEAGHER
          Seems I'll be doing you a service
          then, Lieutenant. Sooner it's out
          of the granary sooner you get your
          men back to Dublin.

Sinclair nods.

                    SINCLAIR
          Somewhat of a powder keg this
          country. Don't you think? Won't
          take much to make it explode.

Meagher does not take the bait.

> MEAGHER
> I've a feeling Juno wants to stretch her legs. What do you say to a race? It's always such a pleasure to beat an Englishman.

> SINCLAIR
> Boasting, Sir, is one of the great failures of your nation, as you are about to learn. First to vault the manor house gates wins?

Meagher nods and whooping the two exuberant young men spur their mounts into a flat out gallop.

EXT. CAHIR. UPPER ROAD TO CAHIR HOUSE - DAY

WS: Thunder of hooves as Meagher and Sinclair gallop along the road - jockeying for position between the narrow HEDGEROWS.

ANGLE: Around the bend the Shanahan family, disconsolate and furious straggle home.

ANGLE: Sinclair edges up on Meagher - then neck and neck - then - advantage Sinclair.

ANGLE: The youngest Shanahan child is running ahead of the other's. His mother hears the approaching horses and calls out to him. He ignores her.

ANGLE: Meagher urges Juno on.

HIGH ANGLE: The Horses sweep around the bend.

ANGLE: The Child will be crushed by the horses. Sinclair sees but can't rein in.

ANGLE: Fergal seizes the child, thrusting him out of the way of Sinclair and grabbing at his horse's BRIDLE.

> FERGAL
> Redcoat scum! Get yer foot off our necks and get back to England!

ANGLE: delighted, Meagher, seizes the moment to streak ahead.

Sinclair breaks free and gallops in pursuit.

Fergal stares after him consumed with anger and frustration.

EXT. CAHIR HOUSE. LODGE AND GATES.

Laughing gleefully Meagher jumps Juno over the gate. He wheels around as Sinclair arrives and reins in.

It's clear that under different circumstances these two young men could be firm friends.

                    MEAGHER
          Ahh! Victory! Nothing smells as
          sweet.

Sinclair grins.

                    SINCLAIR
          Not fair! I do not concede your
          victory. I was waylaid!

                    MEAGHER
          So, fairness matters to you
          Lieutenant?

                    SINCLAIR
          Indeed it does. Is that not natural
          enough?

                    MEAGHER
          So you must concede then, that
          unfairness and injustice may make
          any red blooded man's blood boil?

Sinclair sees where this might go.

                    SINCLAIR
          Yes. I concede that.

Meagher pounces.

                    MEAGHER
          Then, Lieutenant, you understand
          how every Irishman worth the name,
          feels about the injustice heaped
          upon us by a union with England we
          did not choose! Buying and selling
          grain is not the issue. Injustice
          is.

A beat. Sinclair is man enough to acknowledge he has been bested.

                    SINCLAIR
          Nicely done, Sir. May I know your
          name?

                    MEAGHER
          Thomas Francis Meagher. Of
          Waterford.

Sinclair looks at him a beat.

                    SINCLAIR
          Well, Mister Meagher, whilst I hold
          the King's commission I pray that
          fate never pits us one against the
          other.

                    MEAGHER
          Fate just sets the stage. I don't
          fear it. It's the actions of men
          concern me more, lieutenant.

They hold each other's look for a beat.

EXT: CAHIR. PARISH CHURCH AND MANSE - DAY

The distant sound of raised voices. Father Cleary pops his head out of the surprisingly attractive GEORGIAN MANSE. He purses his lips - worried.

ANGLE: At the bottom of the churchyard Dillon and other VILLAGERS buzz with mixed emotions amongst which are anger and fear. Sean (57), Fergal's Father, (a man mountain and by his intimidating looks has seen a brawl or two), and a smallholder holds forth.

                    SEAN
          Without the wheat stored in the
          granary, we'll never survive the
          winter.

A TEENAGER speaks out.

                    RONAN
          Time to shoot Lady Mangan and burn
          Cahir House to a cinder!

Assenting voices. Dillon stares him down.

                    DILLON
          That's your answer, is it, Ronan?
          Shoot down a defenseless woman and
          burn her home?

An angry silence. Then raised voices. People are beginning to take sides. Dillon turns to Neall.

                    DILLON (CONT'D)
          Neall, go fetch your Da.

ANGLE: Cleary turns back towards the house, where his Housekeeper has appeared. She has a slight cast in one eye.

> FATHER CLEARY
> Mrs O'DONNELL! I've to scoot up to
> the Manor, sharpish. Tell Padriag
> I'll be back presently.

With a quick glance at the growing crowd he hurries off.

EXT. CAHIR. CAHIR HOUSE. HALLWAY AND STAIRS - DAY

Mrs Walsh and Grace descend the stairs towards the, cavernous main hall, with hanging antique tapestries and period furniture. Every bit the opposite of the plain cottages of the Irish people.

> MRS WALSH
> Delorey, is it truly your intention
> to find a position here?

> GRACE
> I was thinking a wage would come in
> handy. Mrs Walsh.

> MRS WALSH
> Thinking is it?

She gives a disapproving sniff.

> MRS WALSH (CONT'D)
> I'll not bamboozle you by telling
> you you've made a good start. But
> then there's no knowing with her
> Ladyship.

And she disappears to her quarters.

EXT. CAHIR HOUSE. MAIN ENTRANCE - DAY

Thomas Francis Meagher hitches Juno to a POST. He looks up as Grace emerges.

> MEAGHER
> Aah. Please tell her Ladyship that
> Mister Thomas Francis Meagher is
> here to see her.

> GRACE
> She's inside. She has a migraine or
> some such.

> MEAGHER
> I'm sorry?

                    GRACE
          Migraine! It's some kind of
          headache.

She offers: as though he's hard of hearing.

Thomas Francis Meagher is thrown by this odd welcome, but as he watches her descend the steps he is powerfully struck by her beauty.

She stops suddenly, stares at him. He looks at her quizzically.

                    GRACE (CONT'D)
          Did you say *Thomas* Francis Meagher?

                    MEAGHER
          I did.

Grace is momentarily overawed - a moment quickly covered.

                    GRACE
          The Thomas Francis Meagher. Of
          Waterford?

                    MEAGHER
          I haven't heard tell of another.

She smiles admiringly. He smiles back, uncharacteristically lost for words.

                    MEAGHER (CONT'D)
          It seems the name has meaning for
          you?

                    GRACE
          I'm delighted to meet you, Sir.
          What brings you here?

He looks at her, avoids answering. Flirts.

                    MEAGHER
          Delighted? Certainly that's a
          promising place to start, I would
          say.

Grace examines him, sensing in herself and resisting, the stirrings of a profoundly enjoyable attraction.

                    GRACE
          You're quite the image of your
          likeness.

                    MEAGHER
          My likeness?

                    GRACE
          Rather better than your likeness, I
          would say. In the Nation...

                    MEAGHER
          The Nation?

                    GRACE
          Why do you keep repeating what I
          say? Am I that inarticulate?

Thomas Francis Meagher chuckles. Is she teasing?

                    MEAGHER
          Inarticulate is not the word that
          comes to mind.

                    GRACE
          They gave you a much bigger nose.
          The real thing is much preferable,
          I have to say...

                    MEAGHER
          I'm glad you approve.

Another beat. Feeling she has given too much away she adds:

                    GRACE
          I read it avidly. The Nation, I
          mean. It described you as "up and
          coming." Are you?

Again he wonders if she is teasing him. She is - masking her deepening attraction.

                    MEAGHER
          Well, I...

                    GRACE
          It said Ireland would benefit from
          your, umm... "acumen and silver
          tongue if you would only devote
          yourself fully to the cause of
          Irish freedom."

                    MEAGHER
          You read that?

                    GRACE
          You seem surprised?

                    MEAGHER
               Surprised? Not at all...

A sudden understanding hits Grace.

                    GRACE
               You most certainly *are* surprised,
               Sir.

                    MEAGHER
               Am I?

Grace chuckles wryly.

                    GRACE
               You are surprised that a *mere* maid
               can read, I'll wager, and that
               being so equipped should read a
               newspaper and not some milksop
               catechism!

He chuckles in turn and tries a deflection.

                    MEAGHER
               Milksop catechism? I like it! You
               have an ear for a good phrase it
               seems but I...

                    GRACE
               Will you deny what you were
               thinking, Mr Meagher?

Clearly his mind has been read and Thomas Francis Meagher, more and more enamored, decides on capitulation.

                    MEAGHER
               No, I surrender. I plead guilty to
               all charges. I offer my sincere...

But she is not to be mollified.

                    GRACE
               Ah, well now, all that is needed to
               compound your error, is that you
               order me to call a groom to stable
               your horse!

Is there a twinkle in her eye? He can't quite be sure.

                    GRACE (CONT'D)
               Well, for all I care, you may ride
               the mare into the house and stable
               her in the drawing room! Good day,
               Sir.

She moves down the steps. He watches. She turns back.

                    GRACE (CONT'D)
          Silver tongue? Acumen? Ireland's
          hope?

She regards him quizzically.

                    GRACE (CONT'D)
          I'm puzzled.

                    MEAGHER
          You surely aren't the only one,
          Miss, er...?

                    GRACE
          I'm wondering, only wondering
          mind... if the person standing
          before me is, in truth, no more
          than a man who measures everything
          against his position in society?

Her tone is light but her words go straight to his soul. He realizes that he is being most perceptively roasted.

                    MEAGHER
          A common fault. Snobbery cuts both
          ways does it not? I'm sure that you
          know what they say about people in
          glass houses?

Touche. She grins.

                    GRACE
          A person, however who rides what
          must be the finest mare in the
          whole of Tipperary, if not Ireland.

Another grin and she marches off - leaving him more smitten than he could ever have imagined. He looks at Juno, who paws the ground and whinnies

                    MEAGHER
          Jealous, eh?

He chuckles and ascends the steps.

ANGLE: Grace strides from the house.

                    GRACE
          Glass houses, indeed!

She steps out of the way of a well turned out CARRIAGE AND
PAIR driven by a FLORID bewhiskered GRAIN FACTOR, on its way
to the manor.

EXT. CAHIR. FINN'S TAVERN DAY.

Noise from the inside. Neall and a few other children sit
outside. One, Rose(7) reveals a BLIGHTED POTATO wrapped in a
bit of cloth. Neall sees.

> NEALL
> You musn't eat that, Rose!

Her brother Ronan, a tousle headed 17 slaps it out of her
hand.

> RONAN
> Rose!

Tears spring to her eyes.

> ROSE
> Can't I eat the good bits?

> RONAN
> There aren't any good bits. Whole
> things poisonous as a rat's
> dropping!

> ROSE
> What will we eat then?

> RONAN
> I don't know, Rose...

His eyes fall on the guarded Granary that looms over the
square. He ruffles Rose's hair.

> RONAN (CONT'D)
> I'll see what I can scrounge
> inside. Neall keep an eye on her.

He crosses into the tavern.

INT. CAHIR. FINN'S TAVERN - DAY

Crowded. A FIDDLER plays a lively reel near the fireplace,
while knots of MEN sit at tables or lean against the bar.

ANGLE: At a table, FERGAL SHANAHAN, and his equally strapping
father, SEAN, whose nose has clearly been broken a few times.

                    SEAN
          News is bad all over. Every village
          round about is cursed same as ours.

                    FERGAL
          And now that bitch up in the manor
          is threatening eviction!

ANGLE: Worried, Dillon and Tim watch the growing anger.

                    TIM
          You're right, Dillon. This'll end
          badly if we don't calm it down.

They cross to the others.

                    SEAN
          What to do, eh? I've been sitting
          here in front of a fookin' empty
          tankard for well on a hour because
          I cannot afford another.

Ronan has crossed to the group.

                    RONAN
          What about the granary? There's
          enough in there to feed us all
          winter.

                    TIM
          And it's guarded by armed
          soldiers...

                    SEAN
          It's bullshit. I for one will not
          sit by while good Irishmen starve.

                    DILLON
          Tone it down boys.

                    TIM
          We'll petition Lady Mangan. She'll
          not want us to starve.

Sean rises angrily.

                    SEAN
          Tim Delorey I respect you as much
          as I do any man but if that's what
          you believe you're in for a rude
          awakening.

                        TIM
            Lord Mangan always listened and her
            Ladyship'll do the same!

Sean sneers and crosses to the bar, joined by Fergal and
Ronan. Tim and Dillon exchange worried looks.

INT. CAHIR HOUSE. DRAWING ROOM - CONTINUOUS

Lady Mangan lies on a CHAISE LONGUE. Meagher and
MOLLOY(50)the Grain Factor, sit opposite her. Lady Mangan is
very taken with Meagher - to Molloy's frustration.

                    LADY MANGAN
            So Gentlemen, is it to be a bidding
            war?

                        MOLLOY
            Excuse me, your ladyship. I have
            already purchased the grain and you
            have the banker's draft in your
            hand.

Lady Mangan stares distastefully at the DRAFT.

                    LADY MANGAN
            But not cashed Mr Molloy, as you
            know.

                        MOLLOY
            But your Ladyship you gave your
            word. Your promise...

                    LADY MANGAN
            Pish! The only word I feel
            constrained to honor is the promise
            I made to my two dear children in
            London: that they shall not starve.

                        MOLLOY
            Oh! There's very little chance of
            that surely, your Lady....

She raises a finger.

                    LADY MANGAN
            Or... live a life in straitened
            circumstances. London life is not
            inexpensive, you know.

She smiles conspiratorially at Meagher.

                    LADY MANGAN (CONT'D)
          Mister Meagher can you up your
          offer?

                    MEAGHER
          By one shilling a bushel.

Lady Mangan turns to the factor. She's enjoying this.

                    LADY MANGAN
          Mr Molloy?

Molloy sighs, disapprovingly.

                    MOLLOY
          Ladyship, I must vehemently
          protest...

                    LADY MANGAN
          So, Mister Meagher, it seems I must
          accept your offer.

                    MOLLOY
          Wait! I could go higher. Maybe much
          higher. However I will need the
          approval of my principals. I can
          have it by tomorrow mid-morning!

Lady Mangan smiles sweetly.

                    LADY MANGAN
          Then my decision will occur at that
          time, Gentlemen. Goodbye Mister
          Molloy.

Meagher and Molloy rise.

                    LADY MANGAN (CONT'D)
          Oh, Mister Meagher, Perhaps you
          will stay and take tea with a dull
          old widow.

She smiles and giggles flirtatiously. Trapped, Meagher nods.

INT. CAHIR. FINN'S TAVERN - DAY

The Tavern is more crowded, the atmosphere has heated up.

                    SEAN
          So we stay meek and mild and let
          ourselves be led to the workhouse
          without putting up a fight, Tim? Is
          that what you want?

TIM
We have right on our side I'm
saying...

SEAN
Bowing and scraping to her
Ladyship, that's done with, at
least in this village! Done with!

DILLON
Will you let him speak, Sean!

Tim sees he's losing control. He loves these men and is
genuinely fearful for them.

TIM
No one's telling you to bow and
scrape. Use your brains I'm saying.
We'll make deputation...

RONAN
Kiss their fat backsides you're
saying!

DILLON
Will you listen to the man, for
God's sake!

But the door bursts open and PATRICK - last seen arguing with
the Road Foreman enters. Incensed with injustice, he jumps up
on the bar, and the fiddling stops.

PATRICK
Fellow Irishmen, how many of you
have worked on the government's
cursed road to nowhere this month?

A majority of the men raise their hands.

PATRICK (CONT'D)
I just came from the square. That
bastard foreman says there's no
Government money to pay us our due!

Anger and disappointment greets this.

SEAN
It's not just our crop that's
fecking diseased! The whole set up
here's as rotten as our blighted
crop!

Sean turns on Tim.

                        SEAN (CONT'D)
            No one's listening to us, Timothy
            Delorey! For all the government in
            England cares we are corpses
            already.

                        PATRICK
            For every penny the English owe us,
            we will take a fistful of grain!

The crowd stand and cheer, swamping Tim and Dillon.

INT. CAHIR HOUSE. DRAWING ROOM - DAY

Mrs Walsh pours TEA into a slightly chipped, mismatched, Wedgwood TEA SET, but is listening intently.

                        LADY MANGAN
            In London circles, oh how badly I
            miss London, they say the blight is
            a divine visitation!

Meagher is about to object but she continues.

                        LADY MANGAN (CONT'D)
            Ghastly! Makes me ill to think of
            it. Quite terrible!

                        MEAGHER
            Indeed it is. But the divine has
            little to do with it.

She ignores that.

                        LADY MANGAN
            We are all of us very much
            affected.

She waves the eavesdropping Mrs Walsh out of the room.

                        LADY MANGAN (CONT'D)
            Thank you, Mrs Walsh.

She lowers her voice and leans forwards conspiratorially..

                        LADY MANGAN (CONT'D)
            Confidentially, My dear Mister
            Meagher, my dear departed husband
            left me saddled with debts and
            disorder...

She sighs, touchingly she supposes. Meagher is not unsympathetic but would rather be elsewhere

                    MEAGHER
          These are very hard times, your
          ladyship. For everyone as you...

                    LADY MANGAN
          Hard, Sir? They are grim. My
          tenants have not paid their rents,
          my debts are growing into a
          mountain... Excuse me.

A beat. She dabs away a tear.

                    LADY MANGAN (CONT'D)
          This house needs a man, Mister
          Meagher! I don't mind saying it...
          but it does. A young man...

She dabs away another tear, but is observing him intently. He wonders how to exit without losing a chance to buy the grain.

                    MEAGHER
          I understand your situation.

She looks at him winningly.

                    LADY MANGAN
          Thank you, Mister Meagher. I am
          sure you do. You are obviously a
          man of breeding and sensitivity.

Another beat. Meagher pulls out a fob watch.

                    MEAGHER
          Good Lord! Well, I must be leaving.

Disappointed and disconcerted, she smiles nonetheless.

                    LADY MANGAN
          But you have hardly touched your
          tea, Mister Meagher? Another cup
          surely. I want to hear all about
          Dublin. There is, at least, some
          polite society there, I imagine

He acquiesces, earning another winning smile.

EXT. CAHIR. FINN'S TAVERN - DAY

Hubbub from within. Tim leads Dillon into the yard.

                    TIM
          Those boys are in no mood to
          listen.

He stops at fresh shouting from inside the tavern.

                    DILLON
          What should we do? this has to be
          dampened down...

                    TIM
          I'm worried about Grace. She went
          up to the Manor. Could you go up
          there and escort her home. If she
          gets wind of this she'll want to be
          part of it.

                    DILLON
          Your daughter is not an easy one to
          gainsay, Timothy. You'll be knowing
          that as well as I.

                    TIM
          She'll listen to you, Dillon. If
          she trusts anyone it'll be you.

Dillon laughs, not convinced, though he wants to be.

                    DILLON
          Chance'd be a fine thing. Mostly
          she seems too annoyed with me to
          listen to anything I have to say.

Tim gives him a long look. Shakes his head. Much he wants to say but this is not the time.

                    TIM
          If ever a father knew his daughter,
          I know my Grace. Believe me, I do.

The Tavern door opens and the crowd pours out, led by Patrick and powerfully fired up. Dillon nods at Tim.

                    DILLON
          Will you not come with me?

                    TIM
          No, I'm needed here.

A MOB is growing, jostling them.

                    PATRICK
          If they won't pay us what they owe
          us, we have no choice but to take
          it! That wheat is rightly ours. We
          planted it we harvested it! We
          shall eat it!

                        TIM
            Get Grace home, then run up to the
            Granary. I'll need your support
            there, I'm minded.

As Dillon leaves.

                        TIM (CONT'D)
            Dillon! Women warm to boldness.
            Remember that.

He turns to the furious men

                        TIM (CONT'D)
            Boys... Listen... There is another
            way, if you'll only give it a
            chance.

But he is swept up in the crowd.

INT. CAHIR. CAHIR HOUSE STAIRCASE.

Arm in arm, Lady Mangan and Meagher descend the stairs.

                        LADY MANGAN
            When his lordship was alive I spent
            at least eight months a year in
            London or my beloved Paris. He was
            very much older than I, you know.
            So here I am. As they say:
            footloose and fancy free.

                        MEAGHER
            Aah. Yes.

He nods. She misreads his reticence.

                        LADY MANGAN
            Are you really, *really* sure we
            can't prevail on you to stay for
            some supper, Mr Meagher? Now be a
            good boy and say yes.

                        MEAGHER
            No. I have a previous engagement,
            your Ladyship.

                        LADY MANGAN
            So naughty! If you reconsider We
            could cement your deal for the
            grain... amongst other things.

She smiles at him, almost a wink. They have reached the
bottom of the stairs.

                    MEAGHER
          And have Mister Molloy take us to
          court for conspiring against him? I
          think not.

He chuckles. Kisses her hand. She nods seemingly content.

He heads for the door. He turns back, and makes a mistake
that will change his life.

                    MEAGHER (CONT'D)
          Oh! Your Ladyship could help me
          with one small matter...

                    LADY MANGAN
          Anything Mr Meagher.

                    MEAGHER
          A young woman was leaving this
          house as I entered.

Her eyes narrow. In his enthusiasm he compounds his mistake.

                    MEAGHER (CONT'D)
          Rather striking. Long dark hair.
          Remarkable eyes. I wondered if you
          would give me her name.

Lady Mangan , despite herself, feels a powerful and
unforgiving jealousy. She stares at him, all at once
profoundly disliking him.

                    LADY MANGAN
          I don't think I know such a person
          Mister Meagher, I'm sure. Nor do I
          find your enquiry worthy of a
          gentleman...

Before she can continue Walsh and Father Cleary burst into
the hallway.

                    WALSH
          Excuse me your Ladyship, but there
          is talk in the village of attacking
          the Granary and burning it to the
          ground!

Father Cleary nods.

                    FATHER CLEARY
          There is a tide of bad feeling in
          the village...

LADY MANGAN
Then call the military! They do
nothing but sit around eating my
food and cooling their heels!

WALSH
Yes, your Ladyship. My thoughts
entirely...

He turns to leave. Meagher makes a sudden decision.

MEAGHER
Wait! Let me buy the grain! I shall
distribute it to the needy in the
village. No need for violence, your
Ladyship. And I will pay the extra
shilling a bushel!

They all stare at Meagher, assessing what he has just said.

MEAGHER (CONT'D)
I fear that if it is not done here,
and now, then all over Ireland and
speedily, we face an unspeakable
tragedy... and an explosion of
anger, quite as fierce as the
French revolution.

He surprises himself with his own vehemence. Lady Mangan
looks at him, jealousy now compounded by suspicion.

LADY MANGAN
And I discover at midday tomorrow
that Mr Molloy has bettered your
offer and I have been taken for a
fool! Like my late husband. Duped
of my money! No! And no again!

Meagher steps towards her, Walsh advances on him
threateningly.

MEAGHER
Lady Mangan, you'll lose nothing.
More, you would combine profit with
Christian charity. Surely...

Feeling harassed, Lady Mangan says tearfully.

LADY MANGAN
Don't try it. I'm sick of your bog
religion, it won't wash. The law is
on my side. The land is mine! The
grain is mine!
(MORE)

                    LADY MANGAN (CONT'D)
               Mine to dispose of as I choose.
               There's an end of it. Good day to
               you.

She turns and flees up the stairs. Meagher realises the
seriousness of what has just happened.

EXT. ROAD AND FIELDS BELOW CAHIR HOUSE - DAY

Liam Shanahan(9), runs full pelt up the road.

                    LIAM
               Mam! Mam! There's a fight! At the
               Granary! Da says to stay away!

The knot of despairing Shanahan women, look up in alarm.
Grace is with them. Blighted potato plants and rotted tubers
lie in heaps.

                    MARY SHANAHAN
               God help us, what next!

She heads to the road followed by the others.

                    LIAM
               Da said to stay here! He'll be
               coming shortly. There's soldiers
               coming, Mam!

The women stop uncertainly.

                    GRACE
               Liam! Was my father with them?

Liam breathless can only manage a nod. Grace panics.

                    GRACE (CONT'D)
               Oh lord no! He'll be putting
               himself in danger, I know it.

She is already on the run as she reaches the road the sound
of galloping hoofs make her turn.

Meagher is galloping down the sloping road. Grace runs to
intercept him. He reins in.

                    GRACE (CONT'D)
               For the love of God can I ride with
               you to the village! There's likely
               a riot spilling over...

                    MEAGHER
               I know! I'm minded to find a way to
               hold back the soldiers.

                    GRACE
          Lift me up! Me father barely has
          his sight. I must get to him.

The faint sound of shouting floats up from the village below.
A Military TRUMPET sounds the alarm

                    MEAGHER
          It'll be no place for a woman.
          That's a call to arms. There'll
          likely be shooting next.

Grace's fear for her beloved father brims over, she pulls at
Meagher's saddle.

                    GRACE
          Give me a ride, man, or I'll pull
          you down from this horse and ride
          her there myself!

Her palpable terror for her father persuades him.

                    MEAGHER
          Come on then!

He hefts her up.

EXT. CAHIR VILLAGE. GRANARY AND STREET - DAY

ANGLE: BRITISH SOLDIERS form a line in front of the Granary.

ANGLE: The street. A MOB has assembled, brimming with
righteous anger.

                    PATRICK
          A fist full of grain for every
          penny the English owe us, right
          boys?

The crowd cheer their assent. Tim swept along by the crowd,
stumbles. His SPECTACLES fall. He gropes for them. Ronan
hoists him up.

                    RONAN
          Go on home man. This is no place
          for you now.

                    TIM
          I'll never leave another Irishman
          to fight for me.

Ronan laughs and pats him on the back. Tim stares at his
spectacles. One lens is cracked.

The crowd marches towards the line of troops.

EXT. CAHIR. ROAD FROM CAHIR HOUSE TO VILLAGE - DAY

A few stragglers head to the village. Dillon hurries up the road. He calls out.

> DILLON
> Have you seen Grace Delorey?

A straggler shakes his head.

> STRAGGLER
> Might be comforting the Shanahans.

More shouting from the village. Torn, Dillon hurries on.

EXT. CAHIR VILLAGE. GRANARY AND STREET - DAY

The crowd swells. Men hand out LOYS and Pick-Axe handles. Tim pushes to the front.

> SEAN
> You still with us, are you?

> TIM
> Someone has to look out for youse.

Sean laughs, touched.

ANGLE: Granary. SINCLAIR, confers with his Sergeant Major:

> SINCLAIR
> We need a show of force. Get B
> company here, sharpish.

A PRIVATE salutes, and runs off. Sinclair anxiously surveys the approaching crowd. A few soldiers murmur.

> SINCLAIR (CONT'D)
> Steady now!

EXT. CAHIR. ROAD FROM CAHIR HOUSE TO VILLAGE - DAY

Dillon hurries up the road.

ANGLE: Meagher with Grace clinging to his back gallops down the narrow road. Even through the tension the two of them are aware of their bodily contact.

> MEAGHER
> Hold me tight. We're going to jump
> the wall. We can cut across the
> fields.

She holds him tighter.

> MEAGHER (CONT'D)
> Tighter still, or we'll both take a
> tumble. What's your name!

> GRACE
> Grace!

> MEAGHER
> Hold on, Grace.

ANGLE: To Dillon's shock he sees Grace, clinging to a well dressed stranger's back, leap across the low stone wall on a white horse and streak away across the fields.

> DILLON
> Grace?! God almighty!

He stares at the sight for a moment then turns and runs back towards the village.

EXT. CAHIR. UPPER VILLAGE. ARMY BILLET - DAY

B Company are assembling and preparing to march to the Granary. The Bugle calls again.

EXT. CAHIR VILLAGE. GRANARY AND STREET - DAY

ANGLE: The crowd are advancing, LOY'S AND AXES wave.

ANGLE: Sinclair, mounts up. Addresses his men.

> SINCLAIR
> We'll protect the Granary. Not a
> shot fired unless I give the order!

The soldiers brace themselves. The crowd is frightening given there are not many soldiers at present.

ANGLE: In the crowd. Tim forces his way to Patrick.

> TIM
> Patrick. Let me at least talk to
> them, man. They are men like us.

> PATRICK
> Maybe so. But they wear the Queen's
> red and press their boots on our
> necks! Stay out of this, Timothy
> Delorey! Go home to your women.

He not unkindly pushes Tim away. Dillon appears at his side.

                    TIM
          Dillon! Thank God. Tell me my
          girl's safe at home.

                    DILLON
          Aye. Maybe, maybe not.

                    TIM
          What are you meaning... Dillon?
          Where is she?

Before Dillon can answer the crowd surges forward separating the two men.

EXT. CAHIR VILLAGE. STREET BEHIND GRANARY - DAY

Running figures - some excited TEENAGERS collecting STONES. The air is full of catcalls and shouting over which we can hear Sinclair.

                    SINCLAIR (OS)
          I am asking you to disperse! The
          Granary is private property!

ANGLE: Meagher halts Juno and slides Grace to the ground.

                    GRACE
          We can get closer! Please. My
          father...

                    MEAGHER
          Too dangerous!

                    GRACE
          I don't care!

                    MEAGHER
          Grace, We have barely met. But know
          this, whatever happens between us I
          will never *ever* put you in danger.

He leans close to her, they are looking into each other's eyes. A flash of electricity between them leaves her breathless.

                    MEAGHER (CONT'D)
          Do you understand me?

                    GRACE
          Yes.

                    MEAGHER
          Now, let me try to put a stop to
          this brock.

A beat. She watches, heart pumping, as he rides towards the rear of the Granary.

EXT. CAHIR VILLAGE. GRANARY SQUARE AND STREET - DAY

The crowd taunts the line of soldiers. A teenager hurls a stone, shattering a window in the Granary to cheers.

Frustrated and upset Tim rounds on Patrick and Sean

> TIM
> Patrick! They have guns, more of this and they will use them.

The men ignore him. He gives up in frustration.

ANGLE: Edge of the crowd. Grace catches sight of her father, tries to push through the throng.

> GRACE
> Da!

ANGLE: Sinclair steadies his horse. Shattered GLASS showers him.

> SINCLAIR
> Close order! Fix bayonets.

At the run the soldiers form TWO LINES, BAYONETS are fixed. A moment of stand off.

Meagher appears behind Sinclair. Shouting and taunting restarts.

> MEAGHER
> Lieutenant! Withdraw your men, man.

> SINCLAIR
> I cannot, much as I might wish it, Sir. I am under orders. As you know.

> MEAGHER
> If you will allow the grain to be distributed, I shall personally pay for every bushel. I guarantee it.

Sinclair is torn.

> SINCLAIR
> The crowd must disperse, first.

                    MEAGHER
          Let me address them, Lieutenant I
          implore you!

Another flurry of stones. A SERGEANT calls out to Sinclair.

                    SERGEANT
          Sir!

Sinclair turns to him.

                    SINCLAIR
          Above heads! Warning shots only! On
          command! By the line! Fire!

No sooner said than done these soldiers are well trained. A
reverberating crackle of GUNFIRE.

JUNO SPOOKS, and bolts, throwing Meagher to the ground.

Another crackle. A stray bullet ricochets off the STONEWORK
of the CHURCH. Shards of stone fly.

A SCREAM cut short: Rose standing by Ronan, her brother, puts
her hand to her head. BLOOD GOUTS between her fingers. She
falls.

Ronan stares at her. A moment of stunned silence.

Tim is inches from her. He stares in horror at his shirt,
splattered with her blood and bits of brain.

Beside himself he runs forward, his face with its cracked
glasses contorted with grief.

                    TIM
          See! See what this has led to.

He points to the FROZEN group looking the dead girl.

                    TIM (CONT'D)
          For God's sake! For mercy's sake!

He turns to look at the ashen faced Sinclair.

                    SINCLAIR
          Hold your fire.

                    TIM
          Give them the grain!

In the crowd Grace sees him walk slowly towards the soldiers.

Ronan on, his knees beside his dead sister, shakes his head in disbelief.

Meagher struggles up, stunned, watches as: Tim arms outstretched in supplication turns to the CROWD, then back to the line of soldiers.

                    TIM (CONT'D)
          I am no threat! I am here to ask
          you to let us have what is justly
          ours.

No one knows how to respond. Heads turn as the jingle of accoutrements announces the arrival of B company, forming up rifles at the ready. Walsh with them.

Every face turns to watch Tim's slow walk cross the square. Grace too, she dare not speak.

The sound of Tims hobnailed brogues fills the silence.

                    TIM (CONT'D)
          Let us eat!

The crowd echoes his words, his footsteps and the chant make a rhythm.

Grace chants too torn by fear and admiration. Admiration shared by Meagher who calls out to Sinclair.

                    MEAGHER
          Let them eat!

Sinclair is conflicted by conscience and duty. He eyes the approaching TIM.

His soldiers eye him. A young PRIVATE, THATCHER,(19) licks his lips anxiously.

Tim walks on. Footfalls reverberating.

POV: Through cracked lenses we see the soldiers, GUNS leveled.

Walsh feels the tide turning.

                    WALSH
          For God's sake! Shoot him!

Startled PRIVATE THATCHER FIRES. That sets off a sporadic Volley of shots.

Tim falls to his knees as though hit by a hammer - drilled through the chest.

                         SINCLAIR
                  Cease fire! Goddammit.

Grace with a shriek runs through the crowd to her beloved
father.

Stones resume, the maddened crowd surges forward attacking
the front row of soldiers.

Tim spasms, blood gushing from the wound. Dillon runs to him,
a bullet rips into his arm, he ignores it. Dillon props up
the wounded man. Grace struggles through the crowd.

                         GRACE
                  No! Da! No! No!

The crowd fights with desperation to get at the grain. The
English are pushed back.

Patrick bowls over a soldier, and charges at Sinclair.

                         SINCLAIR
                  Hold fire! Re-form!

But the crowd won't let up. Fists keep flying. Fergal knocks
an English soldier out with a right-left combination. Sean
takes out three Redcoats one after another as if swatting
flies. Sinclair fends off Patrick with the flat of his sabre,
but Patrick pays no attention to the blows.

Soldiers see Sinclair fighting for his life with Patrick.
More panicked firing. Bullets rip into flesh, felling
protestors.

This time, Patrick is shot right through the throat. He goes
down in a guttural scream of agony. He stares up at the sky
as blood pours from his wound.

                         PATRICK
                  Our Father in heaven...

He coughs blood, then lies still - Patrick is dead.

The soldiers fire another volley of shots, and finally, the
rest of the rioters scatter in retreat.

Dillon lifts Tim right onto his back, and stumbling, half
running, he flees for their lives. He spots Fergal and Sean
bolting before him.

ANGLE: CHURCH. Fleeing crowd. Dillon, Tim still on his back,
stumbles towards Grace. They are both soaked through with
Tim's blood.

Grace screams, and rushes to them. She helps to gently lay Tim on the steps, cradling his head. He opens his eyes, looks at his daughter:

                    TIM
          Look after brother, sister...

Tears stream down Grace's face.

                    GRACE
          No no Da! I love you. I'm holding
          you. It's your Grace, holding you.

                    TIM
          Grace?

Blood gurgles out of his mouth.

                    GRACE
          Oh Da! My Da!

She can't speak. She looks back at the square. All seems in slow motion and the sound a jumble, Sean strikes a soldier, who tumbles, Another stabs Sean in the shoulder.

Tim reaches for Grace's face. Feels the tears.

                    TIM
          No tears, my own Grace.

Grace is stifling a scream of grief. She feels Dillon's strong arm around her.

Tim whispers. She leans close.

                    TIM (CONT'D)
          Is that Dillon holding you?

                    GRACE
          Aye, Da, It's Dillon.

A gush of blood, bubbles up from Tim's lungs. He struggles to whisper again.

                    TIM
          Grace, Dillon cares for you
          greatly... Take him into your
          heart... If he's not... There
          already... As I believe... he is.

                    GRACE
          Oh da! Yes... he is. He is!

Dillon bows his head to hide his rising sob. Tim nods.

                    TIM
          I knew so... Tell my Anne I love
          her and... I'm sorry.

His eyes close. His breathing stops and he lies still, dead.

Grace screams, pounds the hard stone. Blood drips down the
steps. Dillon puts his hand on her shoulder, but she shakes
it off, screams again.

Dillon looks around - a troop of English Redcoats has formed
in the square and now marches straight towards them. Dillon
takes charge:

                    DILLON
          Come on. We can't stay here.

With his good arm, he drags her away from her dead father.
She is sobbing openly now, overcome with anguish.

DISSOLVE TO:

INT. DELOREY COTTAGE - DAY

Grace, in tears, dresses the gaping wound on Dillon's arm, as
Anne stands in front of the fire, in shock and grief. Clodagh
cries quietly in the corner.

                    ANNE
          My Tim! Oh Lord, what is to become
          of us?

                    DILLON
          I will help you. We all will.

Anne centres herself, finds her strength, turns to Dillon:

                    ANNE
          I know you will try, Dillon. We
          will all be tested doubly now.

The door bursts open, and Neall rushes in, panicked:

                    NEALL
          The English are going door to door.
          They'll be coming here.

                    ANNE
          Can they not leave us in peace even
          at this time!

Dillon struggles to his feet.

DILLON
          If they find me here you'll all be
          for it.

Anne looks around the modest room. Makes a decision.

                    ANNE
          Wait!

She puts out the fire, pushes aside the grill.

                    ANNE (CONT'D)
          The chimney. Now!

                    DILLON
          I'll be burned alive.

                    ANNE
          Just a little singed. Get in!

There is pounding on the door. Dillon squeezes into the chimney. His hair and clothes sizzle.

Anne replaces the grill and steaming kettle over the glowing coals, nods to Grace, who opens the door.

Three soldiers and a Sergeant push roughly into the room. The children cry in the corner. The sergeant nods to his men:

                    SERGEANT
          Search the place!

Grace stands strong:

                    GRACE
          What is the meaning of this
          intrusion in our home?

                    SERGEANT
          Your husband, Tim Delorey, was
          With the rioters. There were others
          with him who must face the law. Who
          else was with him?

Squeezed inside the chimney, Dillon stifles a cough and listens as: Anne comes after the Sergeant, channelling her grief and anger:

                    ANNE
          You bastards! You murdered my
          husband in cold blood. He was a
          loving husband - a kind father. And
          now you interrupt our grieving?

Through the open door she sees Sinclair waiting outside, she turns to him.

                    ANNE (CONT'D)
          How dare you! I curse you and those
          who follow you. Leave Ireland! You
          are not wanted here.

Anne's speech shakes Sinclair. He motions to his men, who have found nothing, and they leave.

As soon as the door closes, Grace runs to the chimney, and helps a coughing, blackened Dillon out. He collapses in her arms, ash and sparks scattering across the cottage floor.

Prelap: A song of mourning and grief as old as Ireland itself.

EXT. CAHIR. ROAD AND CHURCH - LATE AFTERNOON

Tim's body is carried towards the CHURCHYARD by mourners, followed by Grace, Anne, Neall and Clodagh each struggling with their grief. A few paces behind Dillon - arm in a SLING - and other villagers follow, with Patricks coffin. Behind the first group a third - SMALL COFFIN is carried. Ronan follows it his face drawn in grief.

Above them near the crest of the hill a lone HORSEMAN on a white mare watches.

Sound Over: The haunting song continues.

EXT. CAHIR. HILL ABOVE ROAD - CONTINUOUS

Meagher, watches the cortege. His face suffused with the pain of the past days.

He turns to see a boy scrabbling in a ditch at the side of the road. When the boy looks up, Meagher sees that his mouth is smeared with green.

                    MEAGHER
          Are you eating grass, child?

The boy nods. Meagher sighs.

                    MEAGHER (CONT'D)
          Are your parents still living?

The boy shakes his head - no.

                    MEAGHER (CONT'D)
          Who's your lord?

                        BOY
            It's Lady Mangan. Your Honour.

Meagher nods then reaches into his saddlebag and hands the
boy a piece of bread, which he snatches and runs behind a
tree to devour, passing Lt Sinclair who has just ridden up.

                        SINCLAIR
            I'm to return to England. I'm to be
            replaced. Colonel Harrow is known
            as a hard man. Harder than I.

                        MEAGHER
            I don't doubt it. They'll Be
            clamping down now, for sure.

                        SINCLAIR
            I regret what happened. If that
            means anything to you.

                        MEAGHER
            One injustice breeds another
            Sinclair. Children are eating grass
            and nettles! The situation here is
            intolerable! I hope you'll make
            that clear on your return to
            London.

                        SINCLAIR
            You'd make a better job of it, were
            you to come to London yourself.

Meagher looks at him, the idea suddenly appeals.

The SONG swells.

INT. CAHIR. CHURCH - CONTINUOUS

The singer is Grace. Eyes glistening with tears as she sings
in honour of her dead father.

Many in the congregation have their eyes closed. Some sway,
others exhale as though a burden has been lifted.

Halfway through the song, the chapel door scrapes on the
stone floor, and the congregation turns around to see Meagher
enter. His well-cut wool clothes making him stand out among
the congregation dressed in drab, threadbare clothes.

Meagher stares at Grace, captivated by her beauty and
saddened by the pain in her voice.

Dillon, amongst others turns to look at this intruder. Dillon
frowns, feeling a stab of jealousy.

EXT. CAHIR CHURCH - DUSK

The congregation are gathered in groups. Grace stands with Anne above the newly dug graves. She looks up to see Meagher standing alone by a stand of trees. She crosses to him.

Angle: Dillon standing with Father Cleary and OTHERS including Neall and Clodagh sees Grace greet Meagher.

ANGLE: Grace and Meagher stand amongst the trees.

> MEAGHER
> Please accept my deepest condolences. Grace, the past few days have persuaded me that I can no longer be a bystander in my country.

> GRACE
> Does that mean you are to become a man of action, Mister Meagher? The editor of the Nation will doubtless be pleased.

A wan smile through her palpable grief.

> MEAGHER
> I intend to stay here for some days to collect information and later present what I have learned to the government in London.

> GRACE
> And why are you telling me this Mister Meagher?

> MEAGHER
> Because I came here in search of profit, and because of you, found I was a Patriot.

He wants to say more, but this is not the moment.

> MEAGHER (CONT'D)
> Whatever you or your family may need, I am at your service.

He walks away, she stares after him an instant moved by his words.

She looks around to see Dillon's gaze fixed on her and Meagher's retreating back. She looks back at Meagher, when she turns back to Dillon he has gone.

EXT. WESTMINISTER, LONDON - DAY

The austere government buildings sit amidst the soot of industrial London, in contrast to the green Irish hills.

INT. OFFICE OF THE TREASURY SECRETARY - DAY

CHARLES TREVELYAN, 40, the austere and self-important Assistant Treasury Secretary of Great Britain, sits across his desk from English Member of Parliament JOHN ABEL SMITH, an amiable man in his mid 50s, and the dashing LIONEL DE ROTHSCHILD, 39, Jewish son of the famed banking family, elected first Jewish MP in 1847 and both Co Founders of The British Relief Association set up to help the Irish.

At the back of the room, watching it all, is a stony faced soldier, Colonel RICHARD HARROW, 39, in a red-coated uniform.

>   ABEL SMITH
>   It seems, Charles, that the Prime
>   Minister has made you the veritable
>   Caesar of all things Irish.

Trevelyan nods without vanity.

>   TREVELYAN
>   It is a tall order, indeed. The
>   latest reports I have received are
>   not encouraging. I am about to send
>   the Colonel here to restore order
>   to the countryside.

Rothschild and Abel Smith turn to look at the colonel.

>   ROTHSCHILD
>   Perhaps the Colonel can oversee the
>   distribution of our relief food.

>   TREVELYAN
>   I fear our troops will be too busy
>   quelling the civil unrest. The law
>   cannot be flouted with impunity, My
>   Lord.

>   ROTHSCHILD
>   Laws that see food grown in Ireland
>   sent abroad in a time of famine?
>   They are sorely outdated.

>   TREVELYAN
>   I assure you that the preservation
>   of the free market will never be
>   outdated. This unrest in Ireland is
>   (MORE)

TREVELYAN (CONT'D)
an existential threat to the
British economy. To our very
democracy.

ROTHSCHILD
At the cost of the Irish people.

TREVELYAN
They will benefit in the long run,
learn to be self sufficient.
Everyone agrees that Ireland must
modernise. So it follows we must
let this scarcity burn like a fire,
and leave only the greenest of
shoots in its wake.

ROTHSCHILD
It is famine, not a scarcity!
Hundreds of thousands of people are
dying.

Trevelyan pulls back. Abel Smith tries to be diplomatic:

ABEL SMITH
It is an emergency, Sir Charles.
And we expect you to contribute to
the British Association relief
fund. I have pledged one thousand
pounds. The Queen has agreed too.

Trevelyan grudgingly takes out his check book. He just wants them gone. He writes with a flourish, slides it over to the expectant men. Rothschild looks at it, and his face falls.

ROTHSCHILD
Five pounds? That will help only
one family.

TREVELYAN
I don't think free handouts will
bring the needed improvements. But
you can now use my name and
authority. Good day to you both.

Abel Smith shrugs to Rothschild, and they both exit. Trevelyan turns to Colonel Harrow:

TREVELYAN (CONT'D)
Rothschild intends to run for
parliament. If they will change the
law to allow Jews to serve.

HARROW
Is that likely?

                    TREVELYAN
          Nothing surprises me anymore. If
          they allow Catholics, why not Jews?
          But I do fear for our moral fibre.
                    (glances at some papers)
          So, Colonel Harrow? You have had a
          meteoric rise through the ranks.
          What is your secret?

                    HARROW
                    (smiles proudly)
          I was an orphan, Sir Charles, and
          learned self-reliance and
          discipline at an early age.

                    TREVELYAN
          Exactly what the Irish situation
          calls for. You have your mission.

Colonel Harrow nods, stands, salutes and turns to exit.

                    TREVELYAN (CONT'D)
          May God protect you, Colonel.

EXT. CAHIR. FIELDS AND CEMETERY - DAY

A wide field stretches to the horizon. A HOODED FIGURE,
shrouded in mist moves silently towards a LARGE CART, other
MASKED figures wait motionless. The Hooded Figure goes to the
back of the cart and pulls on a toggle. A flap opens.
Emaciated DEAD BODIES tumble out.

The masked figures carry the dead to makeshift GRAVES. In the
distance others shovel earth over the already interred.

ANGLE: Dillon and Fergal, looking weary, emerge from the
sparse woodland. They stop, horrified by the sight of the
burial before them.

                    FERGAL
          God help me, Dillon! If we don't do
          something soon it'll be us lying
          dead in that damn cart.

                    DILLON
          Makes me feel sick to look at it.

He turns away.

                    FERGAL
          And after us, everyone we love.
          Grace and Annie, Clodagh and Neall
          among them. It's going to get
          worse, Dillon.

Dillon looks back at the harrowing sight.

                    DILLON
          God help us!

                    FERGAL
          God didn't cause this, and it's not
          God will make it worse or better,
          Dillon. Is it now?

He walks off, Dillon looks from the heartbreaking sight in front of him to Cahir House on its hill.

INT. CAHIR HOUSE - DAY

Major Harrow, buffed and polished in his new uniform, cranes his neck, admiring the artwork. Lady Mangan and Walsh are giving him the tour.

                    HARROW
          Your house is most impressive, Lady
          Mangan. A veritable treasure trove
          of... umm, beauty.

He smiles at her, making it clear he is referring to more than the paintings. She simpers and says mournfully:

                    LADY MANGAN
          I wish you could have seen it
          before the troubles began. I've
          already had to auction off many of
          my favourite pieces.

                    HARROW
          Luckily, not the *most* beautiful
          piece, Lady Mangan.

She giggles and pats his arm.

                    LADY MANGAN
          A military man with an eye for
          beauty, Colonel? I shall have to
          watch my step, I see.

She leads him through some French doors.

EXT. CAHIR. CAHIR HOUSE - DAY

They stop on a beautiful colonnaded patio. Below, villagers scour the hillsides for any sustenance.

LADY MANGAN
Those are my tenants. My fields
are encumbered to moneylenders but
they feel entitled to make a desert
of my land, nonetheless.

She looks at him waiting for his response. He shakes his head and tuts.

HARROW
I hope you won't be offended, my
dear Lady Mangan, if I say they
remind me of a swarm of locusts.

She's not offended in the least.

LADY MANGAN
Exactly, my dear Colonel! I keep
them on out of Christian charity
and in return, Mr Walsh suspects,
they come to drain the blood of my
cattle at night. Am I right Walsh?

WALSH
Yes, ladyship.

HARROW
Barbaric! Well, that's going to
change, that's why I'm here, Lady
Mangan. Take heart.

She looks at him admiringly.

LADY MANGAN
Oh, I do Colonel. I do.

EXT. CAHIR. LADY MANGAN'S FIELD - DAY

CU: A hand, reddened with stings pulls a wan bunch of NETTLES from the ground.

Grace and ANNE are amongst a group of women scouring the land for nettles. Their baskets are nearly empty. Hunger is taking its toll, everyone is weary and worn. Grace fights to keep their spirits up.

GRACE
Drink nettle soup and dream of a
fine stew, and it'll go down a
treat.

ANNE
I'd rather just eat a fine stew and
not have to bother with dreaming.

The other women chuckle. They look up as they see a GROUP of HORSEMAN approaching across the fields.

EXT. CAHIR. EDGE OF THE COPSE ABOVE THE FIELD - CONTINUOUS

Dillon and Fergal appear, arguing and tense.

> DILLON
> I'm saying loys against muskets is a fool's game, is all! Look what it brought us. More sorrow! There's a cleverer way, if you've a mind to hear it...

He trails off as he sees the action in the fields below -

Harrow's horse rearing near Grace. He sprints towards them.

Grace, red faced and furious, shouts at HARROW, Walsh and TWO CAVALRYMEN watch.

> GRACE
> We're gathering nettles! Nettles, for God's sake! Does her Ladyship begrudge us those?

> HARROW
> Gather what you like, Girl! But this land is private. Trespassing is against the law!

> GRACE
> But it's not against the law to fatten cattle while forcing us into starvation, is that it?

> HARROW
> Don't split hairs with me. You've livestock of your own, Eat *them*.

> GRACE
> What are you saying? We don't have a pig between us, you idiot. All sold. Every one, a month back!

Assent from the other women. Harrow is increasingly irritated.

> ANNE
> You think we choose to eat nettles, you fecking lobster!

Despite their emaciated state the other women laugh and jeer.

> HARROW
> This is your only warning. I order all of you, in the Queen's name, to leave. Now!

Other villagers begin to crowd around Harrow's horse, which begins prancing anxiously. Grace stands her ground, and Harrow raises his crop as if to strike her.

ANGLE: Edge of the field. Dillon runs faster down the hill, but before he can reach Grace, there is a blur of motion as another horse inserts itself between Harrow and Grace.

The rider is Thomas Francis Meagher.

> MEAGHER
> Cease! These women are no threat to you or her Ladyship!

Harrow brings his horse under control.

> HARROW
> You are all trespassing! This land is under pasture, and her Ladyship has had it walled expressly.

> MEAGHER
> The rightful owners of this land are those women, driven from their rightful property by years of blatant legalised theft!

Vocal assent from the women including Grace. They feel that this man and his educated voice are speaking for them, and they want more of it.

> MEAGHER (CONT'D)
> Maybe the Almighty sent the blight to Ireland, who knows? But it's *English* policies have caused its present starvation. The only trespasser here is you.

> HARROW
> This is sedition, and I am ordering you to desist and leave this place.

Harrow unholsters his CAVALRY CARBINE, and points it at Meagher, who holds his ground.

> HARROW (CONT'D)
> Yield this ground, or I will shoot!

Harrow walks his horse towards Meagher, but the women form a tight knot around him.

                    MEAGHER
          Murder me and you will incite more
          wrath than you ever could imagine.
          Is that what you want for your
          first week in Ireland?

Angry shouts from the women prove Meagher's point.

                    HARROW
          I know all about you, Meagher.

He turns to the women.

                    HARROW (CONT'D)
          Beware. When he's taken every scrap
          of adoration you can give him,
          he'll leave you with nothing! Just
          as he leaves the women he seduces!

Harrow's carbine is unwaveringly pointed at Meagher. His eyes glint, this is a man who enjoys killing.

                    MEAGHER
          I will not give ground. Shoot me if
          you must.

Harrow cocks his carbine. Grace looks at the gun leveled at this determined and obviously brave man. She pushes forward.

                    GRACE
          Do you have so little honour that
          you'd shoot an unarmed man over a
          basket of nettles? In front of
          witnesses? Witnesses who will not
          be afraid to testify.

Harrow glares at Grace.

                    GRACE (CONT'D)
          And if you dared do such a thing do
          you not think we would tear you
          into a thousand pieces like the
          vengeful Greek women of old tore
          apart their tyrant king!

Meagher stares at her in open admiration. The women stare at Harrow ready to act on Grace's words. Harrow gives a cold sneer but finally lowers his gun.

                    HARROW
          Saved by a woman, as befits a man
          of your reputation, Meagher.

He turns to the women.

                    HARROW (CONT'D)
          Let me say this. Obey the law and
          you will have no better friend than
          me. Break the law and I will be
          your merciless and implacable
          enemy.

Harrow nods to Walsh, and they and the cavalrymen ride away.

Meagher leaps down, bows to Grace, and overcome with
excitement takes her hand in his:

                    MEAGHER
          You are both brave and beautiful.
          "Like the Greek women of old." Hah!
          You continue to amaze me, Grace
          Delorey.

Dillon pushes his way through the angry crowd towards Grace.
Meagher turns to the open mouthed women.

                    MEAGHER (CONT'D)
          I shall speak of this moment to the
          newspapers. The world at large will
          know that such beautiful flowers of
          Ireland will not bend before an
          armed soldier.

                    GRACE
          We're more like these nettles than
          flowers, sir. We will only be
          pushed so far before we sting.

Laughter and cheers. Dillon glares at Meagher, who looks at
him quizzically. Anne rushes in, Meagher lets Grace's hand
go. Anne embraces her daughter in relief, turns to Meagher:

                    ANNE
          Thank you, sir! She might have been
          crushed. We'll not forget.

Murmurs of agreement from the other women

                    MEAGHER
          Listen, seeing that soldier ride
          away, tail between his legs, minded
          me of the strength that lies within
          you. You stood your ground!

A surge of pride spreads through the crowd. Grace looks at him her heart alight.

MEAGHER (CONT'D)
It minded me that standing together defeats the slave mentality that has held us back for too long!

Some delighted laughter, some fear. Grace is entranced. He is speaking her mind, speaking the very words that have swirled around inside her for so long.

MEAGHER (CONT'D)
It minded me that God above, the God of battles, bestows his blessing upon those who unsheath the sword in the hour of a nation's peril. I'm overawed and the Government in London shall hear of it, and tremble. Women of Cahir, women of Ireland, I promise it!

He salutes them, mounts his horse, and rides away. Grace becomes the centre of excited chatter:

WOMAN 1
Did you see his eyes? Such blue.

WOMAN 2
I wasn't looking at his eyes.

Grace notices Dillon looking sullen and goes to him.

GRACE
He'd have done the same for anyone.

She tries to take his hand, but he steps backwards.

DILLON
The man's a grain merchant and the son of a grain merchant... A womanizer...

GRACE
Dillon! A man may change may he not? If he's minded to.

DILLON
What does he care for us? Nothing except to make him look fine and speak high! I don't need him to speak for me, thank you, kindly Grace.

And he stalks off. Grace stares after him frowning. She waves at Anne and follows Dillon across the field.

EXT. CAHIR. PATH TO VILLAGE - LATER

Grace and Dillon walk side by side.

> DILLON
> I'm sorry Grace. I don't know what came over me.

> GRACE
> Don't you now?

> DILLON
> Umm. That Meagher gets on my nerves I'll admit.

> GRACE
> On your nerves, is it, Dillon?

> DILLON
> Er... As a man, I'm meaning.

> GRACE
> Dillon, are you trying to tell me he makes you jealous?

> DILLON
> No. Not jealous. Not jealous exactly...

> GRACE
> Not exactly. That's good.

> DILLON
> I just want to look after you, Grace. When I think of Ireland hungry, I think of you. I would do anything to help your family.

That touches her.

> GRACE
> Indeed you always have, Dillon.

> DILLON
> The Delorey family needs a man Grace. In these terrible times.

She smiles at him, teasing but tender.

                    GRACE
          And do you have someone in mind,
          Dillon Culhane?

A beat.

                    DILLON
          Er... Well, I do so... have someone
          in mind.

He stops fearful of taking the leap. She helps him out.

                    GRACE
          And doubtles you are going to keep
          it a dark secret. As you have since
          we took first communion.

Dillon stops and turns to Grace, his self doubt lessened.

                    DILLON
          I believe you have feelings for me
          Grace. As a man.

A beat. Then it gushes out.

                    DILLON (CONT'D)
          I love you Grace. I always have and
          always will. I may lack words
          Grace. But my feelings run deep. I
          am loyal and would die rather than
          let any harm befall you.

She remembers another man saying those very words. She is
aware of Dillon's eyes searching her face.

                    DILLON (CONT'D)
          Will you marry me, Grace?

The simplicity and honesty of his words open her heart.

                    GRACE
          Oh Dillon! I've always had
          feelings for you. Of course I have.
          We grew up together. No stranger
          could have the bonds that we
          share...

He knows who she means. He hardly dare ask his next question.

                    DILLON
          Is that a yes, Grace?

She looks at this companion of her youth, suddenly aware of
his simple strength. Her eyes fill.

                          GRACE
                 It is Dillon. Yes.

He is utterly overcome.

                          DILLON
                 Oh, Gracie...

He suddenly seizes her and swings into a wild dance, that has them collapse into laughter.

EXT. THE DELOREY COTTAGE - EVENING

Grace, alone, hurries home. She notices extra soldiers guarding the Granary.

INT: CHAIR COTTAGE - EVENING

Grace enters and stops shocked to see Meagher sitting at the small table. Before him is a small wooden board with THREE SMALL JOHNNY CAKES on it. He has been writing in a notebook. Neall and Clodagh watch him overawed.

                          MEAGHER
                 Grace, your mother has been kind
                 enough to permit me to observe and
                 note what you all will be eating
                 for dinner this evening?

He puts the Johnny cakes into a small SATCHEL.

                          ANNE
                 Mr. Meagher is making a report to
                 deliver in London on what we eat.

                          GRACE
                 That will be a short report. What
                 will London care about us?

                          MEAGHER
                 We shall make them care. This would
                 not feed a church mouse. It's
                 heinous.

He picks up his notebook and satchel.

                          MEAGHER (CONT'D)
                 Grace, may I have a quiet word?

Grace looks at Anne who nods approval.

EXT. CAHIR. DELOREY COTTAGE. BACK YARD - CONTINUOUS.

Meagher comes out, followed by Grace. He turns to her and speaks quietly but urgently.

> MEAGHER
> Grace. I shall not beat about the bush. I see that God has given you a mind of your own.

> GRACE
> I hope so, Mister Meagher.

> MEAGHER
> A mind that has not been muzzled by the opinions of others. An enquiring mind that will not let you surrender to slavery. A mind, in short, that you are prepared to use. Am I right?

Grace is breathless at his proximity.

> GRACE
> Yes.

> MEAGHER
> The mind of a leader, Grace, and the courage of a leader, as I saw this afternoon.

> GRACE
> I did no more than speak the truth as I saw it. Mister Meagher.

> MEAGHER
> Thomas, please.

He stares at her searching her face, questioning.

> GRACE
> What do you want of me... Thomas?

> MEAGHER
> You know what I want, Grace.

She does. He knows she does.

> MEAGHER (CONT'D)
> When I return from London, I want you to come away with me.

She starts to say something, he goes on.

MEAGHER (CONT'D)
Wait. I want you to be the face of Irish freedom. Your voice to sing of Ireland's hopes. Your mind to be the mind of Irish aspiration, your strength to be the strength of Ireland's resolution. I want you to help Ireland be free by awakening freedom in others as they see in you Ireland's spirit. In the flesh.

Grace is ignited by his vision, but Dillon's warning words are in still in her head.

GRACE
Are you making fun of me?

MEAGHER
By God no! I love you woman. Can't you see it.

And with that he kisses her, a powerfully passionate kiss that she responds to. A beat. They stand looking at each other, each trying to deal with their roiling emotions.

MEAGHER (CONT'D)
I shall be back for you, Grace. I swear it. Together we can make Ireland's freedom something unstoppable. God keep you safe in my absence.

He turns and mounts Juno. She watches, stunned.

INT. CAHIR. DELOREY COTTAGE - CONTINUOUS

Still stunned Grace enters. Anne looks at her. She holds up a GOLD SOVEREIGN.

ANNE
He hid this under his plate. In him, God may have sent our deliverance.

Grace nods absently. Anne looks at her quizzically.

ANNE (CONT'D)
Is something ailing you, Love?

Grace shakes her head, but her mind is whirling.

EXT. CAHIR. HARRIGAN COTTAGE - DAWN.

TORCHES FLICKER. A knot of villagers stands around a COTTAGE on the edge of the village. Three bodies - two adults and one child - laid out on the ground in front of the cottage. The collector of corpses, wearing a mask and gloves, slides them into rough sacks.

Grace appears. Mrs O'Donnell wearing a CLOTH MASK stops her.

> GRACE
> Mrs. O'Donnell, what has happened?

> MRS O'DONNELL
> The Harrigans. It's the black fever. Malnutrition they're saying. Don't go near their cottage.

The last body of the dead Harrigans is slipped into its sack.

> MRS O'DONNELL (CONT'D)
> Can we trust even the air not to kill us?

Grace crosses herself, as Fergal and Dillon throw the lit torches onto the THATCHED ROOF of the cottage. It catches fire quickly, and soon the entire building is an eerie funeral pyre.

Grace looks up. Mounted on Juno, Meagher overlooks the scene. Grace turns as Dillon approaches. He follows Grace's look to see:

Silhouetted against the flames, Meagher rides away.

Dillon stops and he and Grace exchange looks.

EXT. LONDON. WHITEHALL - DAY

Meagher, carrying a satchel, walks with purpose through the busy London streets, alongside his friend and Member of Parliament, WILLIAM SMITH O'BRIEN, 43, a warm hearted Irishman. They pass some pretty London ladies in stylish dresses, who stare and smile at Meagher's dark good looks, Meagher doffs his hat and walks on.

> O'BRIEN
> What? The great Meagher isn't bothering to stop and flirt?

MEAGHER
I've other preoccupations, O'Brien.
This coming meeting with Trevelyan,
for one.

O'BRIEN
I'm impressed, Thomas. You're a
changed man.

MEAGHER
No, I had my eyes opened is all.
What I saw in the countryside. The
dead and dying are burned into my
brain. And I came across someone.

O'Brien laughs.

O'BRIEN
Not changed that much then, Thomas?

MEAGHER
She's not made of the usual stuff,
O'Brien. She's a rare thing. A free
spirit in an island grown used to
serfdom. And... I very much fear
she is going to break my heart.

O'BRIEN
Aah! Met your match, have you
Thomas? The biter bit? Been a long
time coming.

Meagher looks at him with a wry chuckle.

MEAGHER
Well, come it has.

O'BRIEN
And you want to win her heart by
freeing Ireland? Is that it?

MEAGHER
In a nutshell? Maybe yes. God help
me!

They walk on towards the imposing government buildings.

INT. LONDON. WHITEHALL. TREASURY WAITING ROOM - DAY

A silent, cavernous space, portraits of past Chancellors of
the Exchequer hang on the walls.

Meagher, O'Brien and Daniel O'Connell(72)the legendary Irish leader - while infirm of body, his passion and intellect still burn in his dark eyes - sit in UPRIGHT CHAIRS.

A GRANDFATHER CLOCK chimes the half hour. The three men exchange looks.

> O'CONNELL
> I suppose that if I was just to get up and walk into the Minister's office they'd put me back in jail directly.

He's hardly finished when the double doors open and a small posse of OFFICIALS enter with TREVELYAN.

> TREVELYAN
> Gentlemen. Mister O'Connell. I am late for a select committee meeting, but you may make your case as we walk over to the house.

The three Irishmen rise, none too pleased, but dealing with it. O'Connell gestures at Meagher.

> MEAGHER
> Sir Charles, I have spent these past weeks riding around Ireland. The potatoes are rotten from the Giant's Causeway down to Cork. And the fever follows the hunger. I have personally seen thousands of corpses tossed like washing in the hedges.

> TREVELYAN
> Oh, come now! I'm sure that is a Celtic exaggeration, Mr. Meagher.

They exit the room.

INT. LONDON WHITEHALL. STAIRCASE - CONTINUOUS

The group appear at the top of the imposing imperial staircase. They begin their descent.

> MEAGHER
> Sir Charles, the only hope is to prevent the export of grain, open the ports to imported grain, and subsidise the price of food.

O'Brien produces a paper from his breast pocket.

O'BRIEN
I have drafted a proposal. It only awaits your signature, Sir Charles.

Trevelyan ignores the proffered document.

TREVELYAN
The market decides. It must be left to decide, O'Brien. Free trade is sacrosanct to this Government. You know that. I don't have to repeat it.

Meagher can't hold back.

MEAGHER
So the market is free but the people are not!

O'Connell shoots him a look.

O'CONNELL
Sir Charles, we also request the government to halt the mass evictions that are worsening the plight of the poor. She is in your hands – in your power. If you do not save her, she cannot save herself. One-fourth of her population will perish unless Parliament comes to their relief

TREVELYAN
Forgive me gentlemen, but if Her Majesty's Government gives Ireland all that is necessary to survive, what is clearly a judgement from God, the Irish people will just come to rely on the British government instead of learning how to fix their own problems.

The three Irishmen all talk at once.

O'CONNELL (CONT'D)
The unjust land distribution in Ireland *IS* a product of Government intervention.

O'BRIEN
Allowing the export of food in a time of famine is... preposterous...

                    MEAGHER
          Or a deliberate attempt to starve
          the population!

Trevelyan sighs, but does not stop descending the stairs.

                    TREVELYAN
          No Sir, it is not deliberate! The
          reality is, however, that the
          famine is an effective mechanism
          for reducing surplus population
          that cannot be fed. Brutal but
          true. The Government would be
          foolish to fly in the face of what
          is a purely natural process.

The three Irishmen look at each other in consternation.

INT. LONDON. WESTMINSTER. HOUSE OF LORDS - CONTINUOUS.

The group approach a COMMITTEE ROOM. O'Connell is leaning on his cane and breathless. They stop by a central TABLE.

                    O'CONNELL
          How far do you think you can push a
          man before he rebels, Sir Charles?

                    TREVELYAN
          I hope that is not a threat,
          O'Connell. I'd hate to see you in
          jail again at your advanced age.

                    O'CONNELL
          My dear Trevelyan let me make it
          crystal clear. I am the friend of
          liberty in every country, class and
          color. My sympathy with distress
          extends itself to every corner of
          the earth to wherever the miserable
          are to be succored, or the slave to
          be set free, but right now my
          spirit is at home, in my own green
          isle and I delight to dwell there
          with a *fed* people not a starving
          one!

Trevelyan raises his eyebrows and huffs. He moves to the doorway. Meagher roots in his satchel.

                    MEAGHER
          Sir, While in the country, I
          observed farm women preparing food
          for their families.
                         (MORE)

68.

MEAGHER (CONT'D)
These are johnnycakes made of nettles, indigestible Indian meal and an absurdly tiny amount of oatmeal.

He pours out the contents of the container - THREE SMALL JOHNNY CAKES - ONTO THE TABLE.

MEAGHER (CONT'D)
Such, I assure you, is the *sole* meal of the day for millions.

Trevelyan is ruffled.

TREVELYAN
So? I could subsist on that. And I keep hearing about the legendary strength of the Irish peasantry.

MEAGHER
This is not the food for one man, Sir, but for a family of *five*.

Trevelyan caught out, stares at Meagher in distaste.

TREVELYAN
Clever ploy, Mister Meagher.

MEAGHER
You doubt my word?

Trevelyan offers no apology.

MEAGHER (CONT'D)
I'll leave these for you, then. To help you focus the government's policies.

Trevelyan looks at him penetratingly.

TREVELYAN
The real evil with which the government has to contend is not the physical evil of the Famine, Gentlemen, but the moral evil of the selfish, perverse and turbulent character of the people.

With that he and his aides stalk into the committee room. O'Connell rises a sardonic eyebrow.

                    O'CONNELL
          Well, he consented to see us. Pity
          he didn't consent to listen to us
          also.

But Meagher is incandescent.

EXT. LONDON. O'CONNELL'S LODGINGS - DAY

A handsome CABRIOLET emblazoned with the ROTHSCHILD coat of arms stands outside the modest lodging house. O'Brien exits with ROTHSCHILD, They embrace, O'Brien re-enters the house.

                    MEAGHER (V.O.)
          Tyrannies have fallen all across
          Europe! In France, in Prague, in
          Berlin. Belgium has freed itself
          from the Netherlands and yet you
          say, hold your hand!

INT. LONDON O'CONNELL'S LODGINGS - CONTINUOUS

A modest room. Meagher is pacing. O'Connell sits by a table, laden with papers.

                    O'CONNELL
          I was once a fiery young man like
          you, Meagher. God knows I have
          spent a life fighting for Irish
          rights. But heed my words. The
          altar of liberty should not be
          built with blood.

                    MEAGHER
          We are nowhere near liberty, we are
          talking of the right to go on
          breathing!

                    O'CONNELL
          Thomas, I have found in my life
          that the cost of violence is heavy
          indeed, not only on the victims,
          but on the conscience of those who
          wield it.

O'Brien enters, hearing the last part of O'Connell's words.

                    O'BRIEN
          Tom, heed his words. The Government
          has far more guns than we do.

                    MEAGHER
          So we philosophise, while millions
          are condemned to death by
          starvation? Led like lambs to the
          slaughter? Are you so different to
          Trevelyan then?

O'Brien bridles at the insult. O'Connell holds up a hand.

                    O'CONNELL
          Let's not quarrel amongst
          ourselves. Eh?

Meagher is unhappy but holds his peace. A beat: O'Brien refers to the BANKER'S DRAFT in his hand.

                    O'BRIEN
          The good news is Lord Rothschild
          has raised six hundred thousand
          pounds for famine relief. The
          Choctaw tribe from America have
          given one hundred and sixty...

                    MEAGHER
          I applaud them. But..

                    O'BRIEN
          The not so good. Her Majesty Queen
          Victoria has managed one thousand.

Meagher throws up his hands.

                    MEAGHER
          Ugh! Mister O'Connell, you will not
          advocate revolution and I will not
          pledge peace. Our positions are
          irreconcilable.

                    O'BRIEN
          Thomas!

                    MEAGHER
          I believe the poor of Ireland must
          learn to stand tall, to embrace the
          spirit to dare, and the energy to
          act. You believe they should kneel,
          cap in hand. On this too our
          positions are irreconcilable.

                    O'CONNELL
          At this moment, Thomas, a call to
          arms would be both senseless and
          wicked.
                         (MORE)

> O'CONNELL (CONT'D)
> No political change is worth the shedding of a single drop of human blood. Understand?

> MEAGHER
> I do, and I understand this: the soldier is proof against an argument but he is not against a bullet.

He crosses to the door.

> MEAGHER (CONT'D)
> From the grandest mansion to the poorest cottage, the inactivity, the meanness, the debasement which colonialism in Ireland engenders must be expunged. And it will not depart willingly, against it's own interests. Will it?

They all know it won't.

> MEAGHER (CONT'D)
> On this too, our positions are irreconcilable and our association is over.

They look at him in shock as he walks out. A beat then O'Brien follows him.

EXT. CAHIR. VILLAGE SQUARE - NIGHT

A FIDDLER plays as Grace sings a rousing, upbeat traditional Irish reel, a sleeping dog at her feet. The villagers, though clearly emaciated, dance together in the light of a bonfire. It's a harrowing image. But for a moment, at least, there are smiles. Dillon sits in the firelight, dreaming of better times and watching Grace.

Fergal and his father Sean dance by with a couple of PRETTY YOUNG VILLAGERS.

The music speeds up, the people forget their cares and whoop and clap. Even Dillon joins the dance circle around the fire.

His feet move smooth and fast. Grace smiles back at him. There's something wan in it that he senses, but he dances on.

INT. CAHIR. CAHIR HOUSE. BEDROOM ROOM - NIGHT

TWO OIL LAMPS cast a pale glow. The sound of the revelry in the village can be heard faintly but the room is occupied by another sound - love-making.

Lady Mangan is giving herself to someone and apparently mightily enjoying it, her legs are wide and lifted in the air. Between is the athletic figure of COLONEL HARROW.

Having orgasmed, he rolls off her onto his back, and stares at the ceiling. A beat:

                    LADY MANGAN
     Richard, did I please you?

                    HARROW
     Yes.

                    LADY MANGAN
     Very much?

                    HARROW
     If you are proposing to ask me for something, Serena, I suggest you just come out with it.

                    LADY MANGAN
     Richard!

                    HARROW
     Experience tells me that at times like this, a woman's adopting a wheedling tone, usually signifies she wants a favour.

                    LADY MANGAN
     Richard, don't be so imperious.

She snuggles into him. A beat.

                    LADY MANGAN (CONT'D)
     I'm frightened, Richard. Walsh told me that Colonel Mahon of Strokes-town has been murdered. Shot in the head, he told me.

Harrow says nothing.

                    LADY MANGAN (CONT'D)
     Strokestown is only ninety miles from here, Richard.

Harrow sighs.

                    HARROW
     What are you asking of me, Serena? This house is pretty well guarded.

LADY MANGAN
Walsh says, some of the tenants
have formed a secret society. He
warned me to be careful.

HARROW
Good advice. But it can't be that
secret if Walsh knows about it.
Don't allow yourself to be
intimidated.

She leans up on one elbow.

LADY MANGAN
I want to get rid of them! All of
them. And I want you to help me.

Harrow sits up.

HARROW
Serena. I serve only one woman and
that's her majesty, Queen Victoria.
And there's an end to it.

LADY MANGAN
But if tenants break the law that's
against the Queen's interest
surely?

HARROW
Whatever you're scheming, Serena,
the answer is no.

LADY MANGAN
Typical! Over dinner it was all
"Poor dear Serena!" "How can I be
of service, dear Serena?" Now
you've got what you wanted it's,
"There's an end of it!" "The answer
is no!" Blah! Blah! How could I
have been so stupid?

She has given way to tears of frustration. Harrow looks at
her coldly.

HARROW
Don't be coy. We all have needs,
Serena, and we do what we must to
satisfy them. All of us.

She gets up and storms to the door.

                    LADY MANGAN
          I'm not talking about needs! I'm
          talking about survival. If you
          won't assist me I'll do what I have
          to do on my own. Don't think I
          won't.

EXT. CAHIR. VILLAGE SQUARE - NIGHT

The dancing has not ceased, there's a joy in it, but
underlain by a feeling of suppressed hysteria.

Grace watches, slightly distant. She looks up as Dillon sits
next to her.

                    DILLON
          Are you not going to dance, Gracie?
          I understand if you'd rather not.
          Heh! Fergal say's it's like we're
          holding the wake before our own
          funerals!

He chuckles sarcastically. She nods.

                    GRACE
          He's not wrong for once, then.

A beat:

                    DILLON
          Penny for them?

Another beat:

                    GRACE
          Nothing important.

                    DILLON
          Probably Mister Meagher, occupying
          your thoughts?

Caught out, she considers what to say.

                    GRACE
          The Nation says he's splitting with
          O'Connell, that he's becoming a
          force to be reckoned with.

                    DILLON
          The Nation, eh? Does that make it
          true then? That he's becoming a
          force to be reckoned with?

                    GRACE
          It says that the blight has created
          a political crisis that's condemned
          everyone to reveal who they really
          are. For better or worse.

                    DILLON
          I'm thinking I don't need a
          newspaper to tell me that, Grace.

She considers that, then smiles at him gently.

                    GRACE
          Come on then, man. Let's see how
          nimble on your feet you are.

And she leads him into the dance. Anne watches them
thoughtfully.

INT. LONDON. BLACKFRIARS. O'BRIEN'S LODGINGS - NIGHT.

CU a STEEL NIB writes in a neat cursive hand.

My Dear Grace, the nib scratches that out and replaces it
with *My dearest Grace*. A beat: dearest is crossed out.

Meagher sighs in frustration. The door opens to admit O'Brien
he carries more PAPERS.

                    O'BRIEN
          Another donation from Rothschild!
          Jews and Protestants willing to
          save Irish catholics. Wonders never
          cease...

He stops, seeing Meagher's disconsolate face.

                    O'BRIEN (CONT'D)
          Something wrong?

Meagher throws down the pen.

                    MEAGHER
          I know how to end this letter but
          I'll be damned if I know how to
          start it! My mind fills with
          visions of the dead and dying... I
          can't escape them.

O'Brien throws himself into a WORN ARMCHAIR. Closes his eyes
in exhaustion. Meagher picks up the pen again.

                    O'BRIEN
          If you seriously care for that girl
          you shouldn't be writing to her at
          all.

                    MEAGHER
          I shouldn't? That'd be strange way
          to show her I care about her.

                    O'BRIEN
          Anything you write, Thomas, will be
          read by the Government's spies in
          the Post Office. Anyone you write
          to will fall under suspicion. You
          know that as well as I do.

Meagher sighs in frustration, throws down the pen.

                    O'BRIEN (CONT'D)
          In fact I don't think we should go
          back to Ireland at all, Thomas.

                    MEAGHER
          What?

                    O'BRIEN
          O'Connell got a tip off. The
          Government is going to suspend
          Habeus Corpus. We could be arrested
          the moment we step off the boat.
          The gloves are off it seems.

Meagher looks at him grimly.

                    MEAGHER
          So it seems. Yes.

EXT. CAHIR. CAHIR HOUSE. WALSH QUARTERS - NIGHT

Lady Mangan wearing a thick woolen cloak over her night
clothes stands in the doorway with a disgruntled Walsh.

                    WALSH
          If that's what your Ladyship wishes
          of course, I'll do it. But it's
          throwing oil on a smouldering fire,
          seems to me.

                    LADY MANGAN
          It will bring things to a head,
          yes. That's what I want.

Walsh shakes his head.

                    WALSH
          Best to leave people a way out,
          your Ladyship. I fear reprisals.
          That's my honest opinion. His
          Lordship always...

                    LADY MANGAN
          His Lordship is dead, Walsh! This
          is my time, not his.

She turns away, crosses the yard. Walsh heads back inside.

INT. CAHIR HOUSE. WALSH'S QUARTERS - CONTINUOUS

CU: GUN CABINET. Walsh lifts out a PINFIRE SHOTGUN. He regards it with distaste, but proceeds to load it.

EXT. CAHIR. VILLAGE SQUARE - NIGHT

Another log is thrown on the fire. Sparks rise into the air. Some still dance. A STONE BOTTLE is passing from hand to hand as people swig the alcohol.

Dillon now sitting with Fergal swigs in his turn, but his eyes rarely leave Grace, sitting across the fire with Anne, who is looking worn. Next to them Neall, Clodagh, who has a bad cough, and another COUPLE of kids play with a sleepy PUPPY. Anne nods towards Dillon.

                    ANNE
          Have you a date picked?

                    GRACE
          Ma?

                    ANNE
          Grace, I've eyes in my head. You'll
          have to choose, Gracie, or you'll
          lose both.

Grace has been wrestling with that very thought. She sighs.

                    GRACE
          I know, Mam... I'm torn, truth be
          told.

Anne looks at her daughter hiding her weariness.

                    ANNE
          Seems to me you'll be choosing
          between a life here at home with a
          good man. Or choosing another kind
          of life entirely. A restless life.

                        GRACE
            Are you saying Thomas is not a good
            man?

                        ANNE
            Knowing you as I do, he'd be the
            choice I'd wish for you. Though
            your darling father'd be twisting
            in his grave to hear me say it...

She looks up at the sudden silence that has greeted a DOG
CART'S entrance into the square. Walsh sits at the reins, he
carries the SHOTGUN.

                        WALSH
            Celebrating, Eh? And what do you
            all have to celebrate?

                        SEAN
            That we still breathe, Walsh.

                        WALSH
            Boozing too, are we? And I've
            been pleading your case to Her
            Ladyship, that you have no money.

                        DILLON
            Dancing and singing cost nothing.

                        WALSH
            But will it pay your rents? Dancing
            and singing and boozing.

                        FERGAL
            If there were any paying jobs, we'd
            take them in a second. Wouldn't we?

Murmurs of agreement around the fire.

                        WALSH
            So that's your feckless answer is
            it? Dance your way to the
            workhouse?

A beat: The villagers exchange looks.

                        WALSH (CONT'D)
            Her Ladyship wants you all to know
            that she has a magistrate's
            order for evictions against anyone
            in rent arrears.

                    DILLON
          That's the whole of Cahir,
          practically!

                    FERGAL
          Who'll gather her damn harvest,
          then, you Lickarse?!

The villagers are gathering their wits and surround the small
carriage. The Puppy slips out of Clodagh's arms.

                    WALSH
          Her Ladyship will expand her
          livestock. There's more profit in
          them than in you Gombeens, God help
          you!

This elicits the expected outrage and jeering. Walsh stands.

                    WALSH (CONT'D)
          Shout all you like, that won't pay
          the rent either. But her Ladyship
          offers you an alternative, if
          you'll get into your senses and
          listen!

They quieten. The inquisitive Puppy approaches the Horse.

                    WALSH (CONT'D)
          Thank you. To anyone prepared to
          Emigrate, her Ladyship will pay
          thirty shillings towards the
          ticket.

                    FERGAL
          So she'll clear the land by putting
          us in our coffins here or paying us
          to die on board ship. Out of sight
          out of mind, is it? Damn you!

Anger is rising. The horse shies nervously at the Puppy.

                    WALSH
          I'm to warn you also that any
          poaching or coming up to the manor
          grounds with evil intent will be
          met with a bullet.

The Puppy barks, the horse shies, jerking the carriage and
causing Walsh to flop back into the seat. People laugh and
jeer. Excited the Puppy barks, and the horse backs up.

Walsh in a sudden fury fires the shotgun. In the silence that follows people realise that Walsh has shot the puppy. Walsh recovers, tries bravado.

                    WALSH (CONT'D)
          Mark what I'm telling you. You come
          up to the house, be prepared to
          suffer the same fate as the cur.

To a string of curses and children screaming, he turns the dog cart around and heads out of the village.

Anne turns to Grace, her eyes brimming with tears.

                    ANNE
          God forgive me, Grace. I want to
          take up Lady Mangan's offer. I'm
          weary Grace, worn through.

                    GRACE
          Oh, Mam...

She hugs her.

                    ANNE
          What's there here to hold us?
          Clodagh and Neall, look. Wasting
          away before our eyes. I can hardly
          bear to look at them.

Grace looks at Dillon who, concerned has walked over.

                    ANNE (CONT'D)
          What's here for them, Grace, but a
          dreadful death?

As if on cue, Clodagh begins to cough again, deep enough for Grace to cross to her, Dillon watches deeply concerned. After a moment he signals to Fergal. They leave together. Grace helps Clodagh up.

EXT. THE GROUNDS OF LADY MANGAN'S MANOR - NIGHT.

The lights of the Cahir House can be seen in the background. Fergal and Dillon move amongst the cattle. They each have a milk can with a lid. Dillon murmurs to a cow:

                    DILLON
          Come here, my darling.

He is almost caressing the cow by its neck. He produces a small knife and cuts an artery in the cow's neck and immediately raises one of the cans to take the blood.

DILLON (CONT'D)
Just a little blood now, my dear,
and you needn't tell Lady Mangan.

The blood is falling quite audibly into the can.

Fergal approaches a cow and copies Dillon, and again the blood splashes into the can with a loud metallic pinging. Fergal shares a conspiratorial smile with Dillon as the pail quickly fills.

DILLON (CONT'D)
You need to fix them up afterwards.
Just a bit of hair...

Dillon cuts some hair from the cow's tail and uses it to patch the artery. Fergal pats the cow he has just bled.

FERGAL
Tell your sisters to expect us on a regular basis.

Then, there is a shout. Walsh appears out of the darkness, armed with a carbine.

WALSH
Hold thieves!

Dillon and Fergal run for their lives. There is a muzzle flash and gun retort. A bullet whizzes right past Dillon, who keeps running, his precious bucket of blood swishing and slopping as he goes.

Walsh fires another shot, but Dillon and Fergal keep running, with their precious tins as they disappear into the night.

WALSH (CONT'D)
You were warned!

Walsh fires one last shot into the darkness.

INT. THE DELOREY COTTAGE - DAWN

Clodagh has worsened. She looks frail as she huddles by the fire. Grace singing to her softly adjusts a shawl and rough blanket about her. Anne nodding off in the corner watches them, sadly

A knocking on the door. Anne answers, and finds Dillon outside.

                         DILLON
               I've brought you something. From
               her Ladyship. Well, not her
               exactly.

He chuckles as shows Anne a cup of rich, red blood. Anne
motions him quickly inside.

                         ANNE
               Did anybody see you come here?

                         DILLON
               No, of course not. I was careful.

                         ANNE
               Bless you boy. I will make a blood
               cake. May it deliver our Clodagh...
               And hide the evidence.

She takes the blood, and heads to the fireplace to cook.

Grace, still cradling Clodagh, smiles at Dillon. He comes and
sits by the fire. He strokes Clodagh's fevered head.

                         DILLON
               I've hidden a few shillings away -
               If it would help. For Clodagh and
               Neall. For America...

Grace looks at him distraught but grateful. She touches his
arm. An intimate moment.

                         DILLON (CONT'D)
               What's mine is yours, Grace. You
               know that, I hope.

She nods, touched.

                         CLODAGH
               Will we die if we go on a ship. Mam
               said...

Another knock at the door. Grace looks up worried.

                         GRACE
               Walsh - the blood!

Anne hurries a lid onto her pot, and turns to the door. More,
loud pounding. Anne nods to Grace, who opens the door, and
after a moment, laughs!

                    GRACE (CONT'D)
          Why, good morning to you, Mr.
          Meagher! I almost didn't recognise
          you in your plain cloak.

Meagher appears in the doorway - he now wears the simple garb
of the farmers. But he also carries a hamper in his hands.
Everyone is relieved to see him, except Dillon, whose look
changes from anxious to a scowl.

                    MEAGHER
          Blessings on this house. May I?

He gestures to the table.

                    ANNE
          Of course, of course! Come in,
          please! It is an honour to receive
          you again, sir.

This is too much for Dillon, who pushes past Meagher on his
way to the door. Meagher puts his hand out as he passes:

                    MEAGHER
          Thomas Meagher. Any friend of this
          family is a friend of mine, Mister?

                    DILLON
          You'll find plenty here eager to
          buy what you're selling,
          Mr.Meagher. Though I'm not among
          them.

Dillon shakes off Meagher, and slams the door behind him.
Meagher, amused by Dillon chuckles, then opens the hamper
with a flourish and extracts a ham. He hands it to Anne, who
holds it as though it were an unfamiliar child.

                    MEAGHER
          The only good thing that came from
          my visit to London. But I'm afraid
          even Lionel de Rothschild's
          generosity has its limits. The
          conditions all across Ireland are
          too severe. I doubt there will more
          of these to come.

                    ANNE
          I'll make this ham stretch for
          weeks if I have to, Mister Meagher.

She goes to the cupboard and pulls out a jug of Whiskey.

                    ANNE (CONT'D)
          We thank you, and we would be
          honoured to share our whiskey with
          you. It is the last bottle my
          husband made.

                    MEAGHER
          It would be my honour indeed.

She pours him a healthy dram.

                    MEAGHER (CONT'D)
          Let us toast Ireland, garrisoned as
          she might be!

He downs it, nods appreciatively and stands.

                    ANNE
          Will you not stay for another?

                    MEAGHER
          Sadly I have pressing business. But
          before I go, may I have the honour
          of speaking to your daughter in the
          open air?

Anne nods.

                    ANNE
          Of course you may, sir.

Grace rolls her eyes but can't hide her delight.

EXT. CAHIR. HILLSIDE - DAY

The sun is up. Juno is grazing. Grace and Meagher sit on the grassy slope.

                    MEAGHER
          The frustration of trying to get
          the government to listen was as
          nothing compared to the frustration
          of not being able to write to you.
          Did you miss me?

                    GRACE
          No.

                    MEAGHER
          No?

Grace grins.

GRACE
Of course I did, you loon. What do you think? I read about you every week in The Nation.

He chuckles.

MEAGHER
Thank God for The Nation.

GRACE
So is it true, you've broken with Daniel O'Connell and founded your own party?

MEAGHER
Yes. I love and respect the man, for all he's done for Ireland. But too much time in London, and he's lost his stomach for a fight.

GRACE
But you have the stomach for a fight.

MEAGHER
Yes. Under the right circumstances.

GRACE
"The man that can be reasoned with, reason with him. But only the weaponed arm of the patriot can prevail against battalioned despotism."

Meagher laughs.

MEAGHER
You've a fine memory for what you read Mistress Delorey.

GRACE
If what I read gives me hope, I have.

Meagher looks at her.

MEAGHER
By God, we are a good fit, Grace.

A moment between them.

GRACE
Yes, Thomas we are...

She tails off - might say more but does not.

                    MEAGHER
          But?

She wants to tell him about Dillon. But instead she says.

                    GRACE
          If you discover I'm less than you
          think, will we still be a good fit?

He looks at her, thinking. Then he smiles.

                    MEAGHER
          There's something I want you to do
          for me tomorrow. Will you say yes?

                    GRACE
          Even if I don't know what it is?

He chuckles.

                    MEAGHER
          Dare, Grace. Dare!

He stands and hauls her up. They are very close. They might kiss. He decides otherwise.

                    MEAGHER (CONT'D)
          How else do we throw off our
          shackles?

That hits. A beat as their eyes lock.

                    MEAGHER (CONT'D)
          Will you come?

EXT. EXT. COUNTRY ROAD - DAY

The Deloreys are on their way to Mount Slievenamon. Grace and Anne hunt for edible plants along the roadside.

                    ANNE
          No dock-leaves, no shamrocks, no
          nettles! Everything stripped bare!

Her attention is taken by the sight of an OLD WOMAN struggling down the road, carrying a strange burden on her back. As the woman gets closer they see that she carries a body, sewn into a white shroud. Anne and Grace rush to her.

                    ANNE (CONT'D)
          What have you there, mother?

                    OLD WOMAN
          My husband, died overnight of the
          black fever. God rest his gentle
          soul.

                    ANNE
          Let us help you!

                    WOMAN
          We were married thirty-five years.
          I'll carry him the last of our way
          together! Starvation has made him
          light as a baby. The burial ground
          is not far...

She passes the Delorey women and calls over her shoulder:

                    WOMAN (CONT'D)
          The graves are dug already. Waiting
          for all of us.

The Deloreys watch her disappear round a bend in the road.

                    MEAGHER (V.O.)
          Irishmen and Irish women!

EXT. THE MOUNTAIN TOP - DAY

The very definition of a blasted heath - filled today with a
massive crowd. Meagher stands on a cart which has been hauled
up the mountain. There is cheering but Meagher quiets it:

Grace claps near the cart. Dillon is just behind her, but
does not applaud.

At the edge of the crowd, English soldiers watch on
horseback. Harrow listens to Meagher carefully:

                    MEAGHER
          The men of God do not want you to
          fight. I too am a Catholic, but I
          am also a man, and I know the
          rights of man are given by God. I
          ask those men of God, what peace
          have *we* been shown? Should we shun
          the sword? No, for at its blow the
          giant nation of the United States
          has sprung up from the waters of
          the Atlantic, and by its redeeming
          magic the fettered colony became a
          daring, free Republic. As we will
          be!

A cheer erupts from the crowd.

The crowd is whipped into a frenzy. Harrow motions for his anxious soldiers to hold their ground.

>   MEAGHER (CONT'D)
>   Friends, for all they have taken,
>   they have not taken our voice. They
>   will hear it more loudly in the
>   time to come. And I hope you shall
>   hear it now, from the throat of a
>   young woman who sings for us all!

He jumps down and approaches Grace. She looks around, embarrassed. She half whispers.

>   GRACE
>   I told you I would not! I said I
>   would come here only.

Dillon, listens intently as Meagher beseeches Grace.

>   MEAGHER
>   Consider it now, I beg you. They
>   need the hope your voice can bring.

Dillon grabs her elbow.

>   DILLON
>   You must not - look. We are being
>   watched!

He indicates the MOUNTED SOLDIERS. Grace glares at him.

>   GRACE
>   Neither you nor they can forbid a
>   mere song.

She mounts the cart and begins to sing of freedom. (Perhaps "The Harp That Once Through Tara's Hall".) The crowd stares at her, rapt. Some embrace each other, and one or two are silently crying.

Harrow watches stony faced but the eyes of one YOUNG SOLDIER glisten.

Grace is moved by the crowds reaction, as are Dillon and Meagher. When she finishes, Meagher takes her hand and holds it up.

>   MEAGHER
>   I give you Grace Delorey, the voice
>   of our liberty!

The crowd delivers a thunderous ovation. Grace is stunned by the reaction.

Meagher is immediately surrounded by well wishers. Grace remains standing on the cart until Dillon comes to help her down.

					DILLON
			We should leave.

					GRACE
			A long way to come for such a short
			time.

					DILLON
			He's using you, Grace. Can't you
			see it? To furnish his own glory.
			Or worse!

					GRACE
			Or worse, Dillon?

					DILLON
			I see the way he looks at you and
			more importantly the way you look
			at him, Grace.

She can't answer that.

					DILLON (CONT'D)
			Either way you'll end up making a
			fool of yourself. But you always
			were headstrong. You want to play
			with fire go ahead, but I'll not be
			the one to get burnt.

And he turns into the crowd passing Meagher who gives him a sidelong glance. Meagher makes his way to Grace. He grabs her by the hands:

					MEAGHER
			You saw what you can do. I know you
			did. Please, for the love of God,
			travel with me and we shall repeat
			this afternoon and ignite all of
			Ireland...

She glances towards the departing Dillon. Meagher catches the glance, puts two and two together, but resolves to play his cards carefully

					MEAGHER (CONT'D)
			Grace, there comes a time to throw
			caution to the wind and that's as
			true of politics as it is of love.

Butterflies flutter in her stomach.

                        GRACE
            And impulsiveness may be the
            fastest route to hell, Mister
            Meagher, and that's as true of love
            as it is of politics, is it not?

He chuckles despite himself.

                        MEAGHER
            Hell or Heaven, Grace. How will we
            know if we don't even try?

She laughs.

                        GRACE
            Foresight, Thomas, and Reason
            and... Wisdom.

He looks at her quizzically. She is physically drawn to him
and she likes him. He feels it. She is tempted to kiss him
even here in front of the crowd and that frightens her.

                        GRACE (CONT'D)
            If it was only *my* heart involved.
            But there is another... I should
            have said it before. I'm sorry
            Thomas.

She can't go on.

                        GRACE (CONT'D)
            As for politics. I don't want to be
            just a voice. I want one day, to be
            sitting in that Irish parliament
            you are planning to create.

She melts into the crowd. He watches her before giving in to
the adulatory crowd that surrounds him.

EXT. MOUNTAIN ROAD FROM SLIEVENAMON - EVENING

A few GAUNT FIGURES still exhilarated from the meeting
descend the slopes.

Grace and Anne walk together separate from the others. Grace
is thoughtful.

                        ANNE
            Where's Dillon?

                        GRACE
            He went on ahead, Mam.

ANNE
Don't make them fight over you
Grace. Possessive creatures men can
be.

GRACE
It's like a spell. When I'm near
him. All I want is for him to seize
me, to hold me in his arms.

She sighs.

GRACE (CONT'D)
He makes me feel beautiful, God
forgive me! He makes me feel alive,
makes me feel that anything is
possible.

ANNE
And Dillon?

GRACE
I don't know, Mam. It feels right
to be with him. That it's as it
should be. But sometimes I look at
him and wonder if I know him at
all. Who he really is.

ANNE
Minds me of your father. All those
years together and I never knew he
had the courage to face death like
he did.

The clatter of HORSES draws her attention. HARROW AND HIS
TROOP are returning home. She follows them with her eyes.

ANNE (CONT'D)
Is it only a confrontation shows us
who we really are, I'm wondering?

They round a corner and stop aghast as THREE CARTS carrying
SKELETAL corpses, and followed by a straggle of emaciated
children, unload the dead into a MASS GRAVE. Father Cleary,
stands near the cart murmuring a prayer.

ANNE (CONT'D)
Father? If it's a God of mercy that
we worship in that church of yours
why does he stay silent? I'll not
attend another mass until you can
answer that.

They hurry away as we linger on the desolate, silent, burial.

INT. CAHIR. CAHIR HOUSE. KITCHEN - NIGHT

Mrs Walsh is surveying the COOKS. Under her beady eye they baste TWO HUGE GEESE and boil VEGETABLES from the kitchen garden.

INT. CAHIR HOUSE. STUDY - CONTINUOUS.

Walsh is standing before a large DESK, behind it sits Lady Mangan. There are sounds of laughter and MALE VOICES from the nearby Salon.

> WALSH
> It seems, your Ladyship, that only two families have taken up your offer of emigration. The others are stubborn.

Lady Mangan sighs in frustration.

> LADY MANGAN
> Stubborn and feckless! And Mister Meagher. Have you news of him?

> WALSH
> He's hither and thither, stirring things up.

> LADY MANGAN
> Encouraging lawlessness, you are saying?

> WALSH
> I'm saying, they're ready to attack the granary again, only it's too well defended.

Lady Mangan smiles grimly, her mind working.

> LADY MANGAN
> Walsh, I would like you to deliver Mister Molloy's grain to him directly in Waterford, tomorrow.

> WALSH
> Tomorrow, Your Ladyship?

> LADY MANGAN
> The poor man has paid for it, Walsh.

                    WALSH
          It's too dangerous. It will be
          undefended. It will certainly be
          attacked.

                    LADY MANGAN
          Yes. Attacked, Walsh, almost
          certainly. However Mister Molloy
          wants what he has purchased.

                    WALSH
          But your Ladyship...

                    LADY MANGAN
          It will also be defended. That will
          be all Walsh.

He wants to say more but she waves him away. She arranges
some papers on her desk, then crosses to the MIRROR and
musses her hair, sniffing at a little BOTTLE of AMMONIA she
simpers at herself then picks up the LITTLE PEKINESE from its
basket and exits.

INT. CAHIR. CAHIR HOUSE. SALON - LATER

Raucous laughter dies down as the doors open and a TEARFUL
Lady Mangan enters

TWO SUBALTERN's jump to their feet, Colonel HARROW remains
seated in a large WING BACK armchair.

                    LADY MANGAN
          Oh, it's too awful! I'm sorry but I
          feel quite faint...

She flops onto the sofa. A subaltern pours her GLASS OF
MADEIRA.

                    LADY MANGAN (CONT'D)
          Walsh has just brought such
          shocking news. There is to be an
          attack...

Harrow rolls his eyes.

                    HARROW
          Attack? Where, pray, Lady Mangan?

Lady Mangan dabs at her eyes.

                    LADY MANGAN
          Not where.. On. On the grain. I
          shall be ruined. No matter... I'm
          sure my ruin is of little account!

She lies back on the chaise, hands to her eyes. A beat The subalterns look at Harrow.

                    LADY MANGAN (CONT'D)
          Walsh, tells me that Mister Meagher
          is likely behind it!

Harrow sits up.

                    HARROW
          Meagher, you say?

                    LADY MANGAN
          So Walsh has informed me. He is
          quite beside himself with worry. I
          said I shall accompany him...

                    HARROW
          Accompany him?

                    LADY MANGAN
          The Grain has been purchased and
          must be delivered... though we
          shall both probably be shot in the
          head like poor dear Colonel Mahon.

Harrow sees the manipulation and wonders if it might be useful to him. Lady Mangan, sighs deeply.

                    LADY MANGAN (CONT'D)
          But no matter, I say, why should a
          poor woman's travails be of any
          concern, unless...

Harrow waits.

                    LADY MANGAN (CONT'D)
          Sir Charles Trevelyan is uncle to
          my dear friend Dottie Harewood,
          perhaps she will speak to him on my
          behalf.

Harrow absorbs that, quite admiring how the card has been played.

INT. CAHIR. CAHIR HOUSE. LADY MANGAN'S BEDROOM - NIGHT

Harrow is taking Lady Mangan from behind, each stroke an odd mixture of pleasure and anger.

                    HARROW
          You are a little Viper... Do you
          know that! A delicious little...
          Viper!

She gasps at his movements, enjoying them and his words.

                    LADY MANGAN
          Yes... Delicious... Aren't I just?

EXT. CAHIR. STREET AND DELOREY COTTAGE - DAY

Dawn sun. Neall and a COUPLE of scrawny CHILDREN hurtle down the street.

                    NEALL
          Mam, they're moving the grain!

Doors up and down the street open, people begin to assemble. Anne and Grace appear from the doorway.

EXT. CAHIR. GRANARY AND SQUARE - DAY

A crowd assembled. The GRANARY DOORS ARE OPEN, the soldiers are gone. Fergal appears in the doorway.

                    FERGAL
          They've taken it all. Not a feckin'
          grain left!

Murmurs of fury. Sean turns to Neall.

                    SEAN
          Were there soldiers with the carts?

                    NEALL
          Two dragoons, is all. Plus the
          carters and Mister Walsh.

                    GRACE
          They'll be taking the Waterford
          road. If we go over the hill we can
          cut them off!

Cries of approval, people begin to run. Dillon steps in front of Grace.

                    DILLON
          No. Grace it'll be some kind of
          trap!

                    GRACE
          Maybe, maybe not. I've had enough
          of caution, Dillon. Meagher is
          right we've to throw off our
          chains.

Dillon swallows his hurt. He's worried for Grace, Annie and the others.

                    DILLON
          Not like this. Not with violence
          Grace! We've to do it on our terms
          not theirs...

                    GRACE
          Like my darling Father are you?
          Putting up with anything till he
          let them shoot him down!

She is marching with the others. Dillon sees it's hopeless.

                    GRACE (CONT'D)
          You want to be helpful. Stay and
          keep Neall close, watch him and
          Clodagh!

Dillon is in a torment.

                    NEALL
          Aww, Mam.

                    ANNE
          STAY with Dillon, or I'll smack you
          upside the head!

She joins her daughter, hurrying up the street with the others. Dillon watches, frustrated. He turns to Neall.

                    DILLON
          Neall, if I put you and Clodagh in
          care of Mrs Crean, while I go after
          your Mam, do you promise you'll
          stay in here in the village?

                    NEALL
          Why?

                    DILLON
          Because it's what your Mam wants.

And he grabs the pleading boy by his collar and propels him down the street.

EXT. WATERFORD ROAD - DAY

The angry mob of villagers, led by Grace, Fergal and Sean now wielding pikes and farm tools, has gathered on the road.

THREE CARTS appear on the brow of the hill. Walsh, some CARTERS and TWO MOUNTED DRAGOONS escort them .

The starving and incensed Villagers surge forward. Grace leads them as they block the road.

                    GRACE
          That's our wheat, our rye, our
          barley! We sowed it, we worked to
          get it out of the ground, and now
          it's shipped off to England to feed
          anyone but us.

The villagers cheer. Walsh rides ahead, cradling his SHOTGUN.

                    WALSH
          Make way! This is Lady Mangan's
          property.

                    GRACE
          You make way. We must eat, for the
          love of God!

Walsh points the gun at Grace.

                    WALSH
          This is the queen's highway.
          Obstructing our progress is a
          felony!

                    GRACE
          You shoot me, and you won't make it
          out of here alive.

                    FERGAL
          Put it down, Walsh!

Walsh looks at the advancing villagers, and turns and falls back. The villagers cheer and rush forward.

Walsh stops beyond the wagon, and turns his horse to watch.

Grace waves the others on, and they rush up to the grain wagon. The lead horses of the wagon tug, spooked, then rear up. The wagon driver struggles to control them. Some of the bags of grain fall, split, and out pours precious sustenance. Villagers rush to scoop it up.

Grace jumps up on the wagon, and throws more grain down to the desperate people. Walsh watches.

Dillon appears.

                    DILLON
          Grace! There are more soldiers on
          the road! I saw them.

Grace jumps down.

                    GRACE
          Where's Neall, man!

                    DILLON
          Safe with Mrs Crean...

Shouts from the villagers. A TROOP of red-coated soldiers on horseback crests the ridge above them. Harrow in the lead, commands his men:

                    HARROW
          Flat of your sabres unless
          endangered!

The villagers look up to see the troop descending.

                    GRACE
          Fall back! Take the grain and run!

Harrow forges ahead.

                    HARROW
          Charge!

Then: to Grace's and Dillon's horror Neall appears, running to the CARTS to get grain.

                    GRACE
          Neall! My God! Dillon?

Dillon is as shocked as Grace, in tandem they run towards the carts, Neall and the charging soldiers.

                    GRACE (CONT'D)
          Neall! Run!

Neall freezes, as the horsemen descend like furies. The villagers bolt in every direction, panicked.

Dillon grabs a PIKE and Fergal and Sean band together to stop the charge. A few others join them but they are desperately outnumbered.

                    DILLON
          Stick together boys!

The horsemen descend, knocking down villagers left and right.

                    GRACE
          Neall!

Sean gets in a good swing that knocks one soldier off his saddle. But another catches Sean in the head, knocking him down in a spray of blood.

Dillon fends of a soldier threatening Grace, the two tumble to the ground as Grace is knocked sideways by a REARING HORSE.

                    GRACE (CONT'D)
          Neall!

But she can see nothing through the mess of hooves, soldiers and fighting villagers.

Harrow rides hard into Dillon, smacking at him with his sabre. Dillon fights him off, but Harrow wheels around, comes again, and this time Dillon is slashed across the cheek and crumples.

The wagon horses panic, rear up again, and start running. The wagon driver can't stop them, but holds on for dear life.

The wagon thunders ahead, right at Neall.

Grace watches in horror as Neall is trampled under the wagon. She screams, but her voice is drowned in the melee.

The rest of the villagers run for their lives. The mounted soldiers overtake them, kicking and beating them.

Grace dives down next to Neall. His badly beaten body is limp in her arms. He is dead.

Only a few villagers are still able to run. Harrow pulls out his CARBINE, aims at the departing backs, but then fires a shot into the air.

                    HARROW
          I think we've made our point,
          gentlemen.

He wheels around, rides back toward his troop, past the fallen villagers, writhing in the dirt. Sean, on his hands and knees, spits blood into the dirt, then dares to look up:

Harrow passes Sean, casually sword smacks him. Sean falls.

Grace, out of her mind, shakes Neall's limp body. Anne sees her dead son, and wails as she rushes towards him. Grace sees a frantic Dillon crossing to her.

                    GRACE
          Could you not even do that little
          thing, Dillon, to look after this
          child? Could you not do even that?

Dillon stops, horror struck and mortified. Anne seizes NEALL'S limp body from Grace who dissolves into tears. A tableau of grief.

> DILLON
> God forgive me, but this was not my doing, Grace! It was violence led to this. I warned you, Grace. You know I did...

Grace swings around, incandescent with despair and fury.

> GRACE
> No, Dillon it was injustice did this! It was cruelty did this. It was greed did this! It was arrogance did this! It was SUBMISSIVENESS did this!

> DILLON
> Grace! Please...

> GRACE
> Get out of my sight Dillon Culhane! If you can't stand up for us like a man, get out of my sight!

In floods of tears she turns to Anne crouched sobbing over Neall's blooded body.

Fergal stands next to Dillon who stares at the tableau, his heart crushed beyond mending. He turns away shoulders slumped, Fergal follows him.

EXT. CAHIR. WOODS ABOVE THE MANOR HOUSE - EVENING

Dillon sits on a rotting stump.

> DILLON
> I'll never get her words out of my head, Fergal as long as I live they'll be reverberating in my brain.

Fergal looks at him quizzically.

> FERGAL
> There's a way they can be stilled.

> DILLON
> What can I say to her that'll matter...

                    FERGAL
          Nothing. It's deeds will win her
          back to you, Dillon.

Dillon looks at him, intrigued.

INT. CAHIR. DELOREY COTTAGE - NIGHT

Keening, ceremonial mourning, is in progress for Neall, whose body lies, battered, on the table. Anne, Clodagh and Grace are there as well as some NEIGHBOURS and Father Cleary.

                    FATHER CLEARY
          Our dear child Neall Delorey has
          been taken from us to rest with the
          angels... and we must dig deep to
          find the strength to bear God's
          inscrutable will.

                    GRACE
          Is it God's will then and not man's
          malice at play here, father? Do
          you believe that truly?

                    FATHER CLEARY
          Dear Grace, redemption is the child
          of suffering. We cannot let grief
          separate us from closeness to our
          merciful God...

                    GRACE
          Yesterday at that charnel house on
          the Mountain, my mother asked you a
          question. You are not welcome here
          unless you can answer it.

The blasphemy, the challenge to the priest's word, hangs in the air.

A beat: Women cry. Father Cleary says gently:

                    FATHER CLEARY
          Let us pray, my brethren, for the
          repose of the soul of Neall
          Delorey.

Anne goes to her daughter, and takes her hand, finding it in herself to provide comfort in this terrible time. She hugs Grace tightly.

The recital of the rosary begins. Grace, Anne, and Clodagh pray along.

Suddenly, Lady Mangan appears bowing her head under the low door lintel. Walsh follows her. The Rosary stops, at this alien presence. Tension soars. Lady Mangan looks around.

> LADY MANGAN
> I come as a mother, Mrs Delorey. It must be an unbearably tragic thing to lose one so young. Please accept my sympathies.

Anne stares at her battling her soul searing grief.

> ANNE
> You are a brave woman, Lady Mangan, or a foolhardy one coming here! If you'd have had half the tenderness of spirit of the late Lord Mangan, my son would still be alive. Please now go away from here!

> LADY MANGAN
> It was a tragic accident. Quite unintentional, Mrs Delorey, please, please, believe that.

She's convincing, but the mourners are far from won over.

> GRACE
> Those soldiers charged without warning!

> LADY MANGAN
> Because theft was being committed. You were stealing, to be blunt. Both a legal crime and a mortal sin. As I am sure Father Cleary would agree.

Cleary is struggling with this situation and the way it is exposing him.

> FATHER CLEARY
> It is your Ladyship. Though common charity demands the amelioration of the circumstances that bring...

Grace angrily interrupts the platitudes.

> GRACE
> My brother was innocent! He just wanted food for his family! That's no crime. The crime was selling it while we were in need.

Lady Mangan purses her lips. The atmosphere is souring and tension mounting rapidly. Walsh coughs discreetly. Lady Mangan takes a breath.

> LADY MANGAN
> Mrs Delorey, I have come in a state of some distress, and in spirit of compromise, and to make amends.

They look at her, wondering whether to give her the benefit of the doubt. After a beat, Lady Mangan proceeds.

> LADY MANGAN (CONT'D)
> Some weeks ago I offered to pay a certain sum towards the cost of emigration. In honour of your pain and suffering I would be prepared to offer you the full fare. For all your family and a small sum towards making a new beginning.

This is greeted by a shocked silence. Grace stares at Anne, speechless. Anne stands: grief turning to cold fury.

> ANNE
> I've followed your rules all my life. Been subject too to the hypocrisy that exists even within some of my own class 'cos of my colour. And what has been my reward? Creels full of rotting potatoes, and a husband and son who will now join them in the earth! And now you come like carrion to feed on the corpses and take advantage of our grief!

> LADY MANGAN
> No. I am offering you a generous way out of quite impossible circumstances!

Anne can barely control herself.

> ANNE
> Count yourself lucky I don't hold a carving knife in my hand, woman. Because as God is my witness I would plunge it directly into your black heart! Get out of my house!

Lady Mangan looks like she might say more. Walsh tugs at her elbow.

                    LADY MANGAN
            Well, my condolences to this house.

She leaves, followed by Walsh. Anne and Grace take up the
keen of grieving again.

After a second, Cleary quietly exits.

EXT. CAHIR. STREET AND DELOREY COTTAGE - NIGHT

Cleary hurries in the gloom to catch up with Lady Mangan and
Walsh as they climb into the Dog Cart

                    FATHER CLEARY
            Lady Mangan! Mister Walsh!

They stop and turn to the priest.

                    FATHER CLEARY (CONT'D)
            Their hearts are wounded, but they
            will find solace in God, and come
            to consider your generous offer.

                    LADY MANGAN
            Let's hope so Father Cleary.
            I did not want it to come to this.

                    FATHER CLEARY
            Of course not your ladyship. No one
            in their senses would want any of
            this.

                    LADY MANGAN
            Thank you, Father Cleary. You make
            me feel much better.

                    WALSH
            Oh, my God!

He points. On the hillside a RED GLOW is staining the cloudy
night sky.

                    LADY MANGAN
            Walsh! What is it?

                    WALSH
            Cahir House, your Ladyship. It's on
            fire!

EXT: CAHIR. CAHIR HOUSE - NIGHT.

FLAMES leap into the sky. SOLDIERS and SERVANTS organise a
BUCKET CHAIN from the stables and rush them to the burning
WEST WING.

ANGLE: Hidden amongst the TREES Dillon and Fergal watch their handiwork.

                    FERGAL
          God forgive me, but it makes my
          heart feel good to see it burn.

                    DILLON
          Mine too. Fergal, they'll make us
          pay a heavy price for this I'm
          thinking.

They watch the commotion and the flames for a beat.

                    FERGAL
          Come on man, let's go.

They disappear into the woods.

EXT. CAHIR. ROAD BELOW CAHIR HOUSE

                    FERGAL
          Best head home separately, Dillon,
          before we're spotted.

He vaults over LOW wall and vanishes into the night. Dillon take a last look at the burning house.

                    DILLON
          God forgive me.

Torn with a kind of regret Dillon turns, and following a different path to Fergal, disappears amongst the trees. Not seeing: TWO FEMALE FIGURES hunched amongst the trees. One who's odd cast eye we recognise as MRS O'DONNELL, father Cleary's housekeeper.

EXT: CAHIR. CAHIR HOUSE - MORNING.

A tearful Lady Mangan and a tight lipped Harrow survey the burnt out and still smouldering ruins of the WEST WING of Cahir House. About TWENTY POLICE are unloading from some CARRIAGES.

                    LADY MANGAN
          This is horrible. Heartbreaking.

                    HARROW
          You set this in motion Serena, it's
          a bit late to mope now.

                    LADY MANGAN
               That devil, Meagher. He's to blame
               for all this desolation. Stirring
               them up.

Harrow restrains a sarcastic laugh.

                    HARROW
               Well, whatever... now's the time to
               twist the screws tighter. If you're
               up for it. It'll smoke out the
               rebels and eventually make Meagher
               show himself. It's a method I honed
               in India, during the Chol uprising.

                    LADY MANGAN
               I fear he's cleverer than that.

Harrow sneers.

                    HARROW
               Oh, he'll come riding to defend the
               village, especially this Delorey
               girl he fancies. He's a man after
               all, Serena, however intelligent.

She nods, appreciating as she does the power women can exert over men.

                    HARROW (CONT'D)
               There's no going back, Serena. The
               Police are standing by. You have a
               court order. Lex Tallonis.

She looks at him questioningly.

                    HARROW (CONT'D)
               They destroyed your home, you
               destroy theirs. An eye for an eye.

                    LADY MANGAN
               I came here with such high
               hopes...

She gestures at the beautiful country park and it surrounding countryside.

                    LADY MANGAN (CONT'D)
               Now it feels like some kind of
               hell.

She squeezes Harrow's arm. Pulls herself together.

                    LADY MANGAN (CONT'D)
               Still, at least my land will be
               legally vacated.

                    HARROW
               And I will catch my insurgent.

Harrow nods approvingly. As they walk towards the knot of
policemen.

                    HARROW (CONT'D)
               Very satisfying.

She smiles - indeed it is.

INT. CAHIR. THE DELOREY COTTAGE - DAY

Anne cooks the last scraps of the ham from Meagher. Grace
wraps a blanket around the shoulders of her sister, Clodagh,
who shivers. There is a pounding at the door. Grace opens it,
and Walsh strides into the hut.

                    WALSH
               Outside! Now! All of you!

                    GRACE
               What? Why? Walsh? My sister is ill.

                    WALSH
               Just get out there, before you
               regret it.

He turns and leaves. Anne and Grace each take Clodagh by an
arm, helping her stagger outside.

EXT. CAHIR. VILLAGE STREET - DAY

Other villagers also spill out from their cabins, as POLICE
watched by MOUNTED SOLDIERS and Harrow also on horse back
move from door to door.

The villagers murmur between each other, casting worried
glances at the soldiers ad police. Grace notices one of the
English soldiers silently crying.

She takes her mother's hand and squeezes it.

                    WALSH
               The burning of the manor was the
               last straw. We are acting on a
               magistrates order, as you know,
               Everyone in this village will
               be evicted.

There is a great gasp from the villagers, and some people begin to cry.

The soldiers part, to reveal two BATTERING RAM's designed to smash the roofs and walls of the cottages.

>   WALSH (CONT'D)
>   (pointing to a cottage)
>   That one first.

Grace and the others turn to see the ram dragged until it is directly outside Dillon's cottage. Dillon emerges.

>   DILLON
>   No!

>   GRACE
>   Omigod!

Walsh looks to the police and nods.

>   POLICE INSPECTOR
>   Do it!

The ram is pulled back and let go against the wall of Dillon's cottage. He screams. He's held back by TWO POLICEMAN. Grace tries to get to him as ANOTHER RAM is brought in, and lined up against Fergal and Sean's cottage.

>   GRACE
>   God have mercy on you, for we won't
>   when our time comes, unless you
>   show mercy now!

At a signal from the Inspector she is hustled behind the police lines. A policeman runs up to Harrow and the Inspector from Sean and Fergal's cottage.

>   POLICEMAN
>   They refuse to leave, sir.

>   HARROW
>   Then they need to be taught to
>   respect the Law. Inspector?

Gloomily the inspector nods. Police converge on the cottage.

>   SEAN
>   I will not be leaving to die on the
>   road.

>   HARROW
>   You will see your life taken.

                        FERGAL
              It will be you taking it, then.

                        SEAN
              I'll not be leaving. Fergal, get
              out, dear boy. Joy be with you.

                        FERGAL
              No, I will not leave without you.

                        SEAN
              As your father, I order you to
              leave. This is my stand.

Sean grabs his son, and manhandles him right out the door.
Two soldiers grab him, restrain him from going back in.

                        HARROW
              This is your last warning. You will
              be injured or die even if you don't
              heed it.

Sean looks at his son, bows his head, and slams the door.

Harrow nods to the Inspector.

                        HARROW (CONT'D)
              I would say he has made his wishes
              plain. Your men may proceed.

An uneasy exchange of looks amongst the soldiers but the
Police proceed.

                        FERGAL
              No! Murderers!

But the police let the Ram swing and destroys the Shanahan
house. Fergal, still restrained by the two soldiers, screams.

The Ram has moved to the next cottage. Cottage after cottage
is being destroyed by the rams, as the villagers wail and
scream.

The battering ram is prepared at another cottage, but the
sound of a crying baby can be heard. Harrow again enters.

INT. COTTAGE - DAY

Harrow stops short - even for him, this is a shocking sight. A
MAN suckles at the breast of his WIFE, as a skinny BABY wails
on the floor of the hut. The woman, listless, turns to
Harrow:

                        WOMAN
              Judge me if you dare, my baby is
              doomed and we have already mourned
              him. I need to keep my man so that
              he can do the work to buy meal.

Harrow scoops up the baby surprisingly gently in his arms.

                        HARROW
              Leave this place. You are evicted.
              And may God have mercy on you.

Still cradling the baby, he turns to leave.

                        WOMAN
              What will you do to him? Put him
              out of his misery?

Harrow stops, genuinely horrified:

                        HARROW
              God no! I will take him to an
              orphanage where he will have every
              opportunity at a good life. As I
              did.

He exits, still holding the baby.

EXT. COTTAGE - DAY

As Harrow exits, his soldiers stare, mouths agape, and watch their commander as he cradles and soothes the crying baby. The parents weakly crawl out of the hovel.

                        HARROW
              What are you waiting for? Inspector
              have your men ram the cottage.

Harrow mounts his horse, still holding the baby, he rides out of the village as the cottage is destroyed.

ANGLE the Delorey cottage. Harrow passes and watches as pinioned by TWO POLICEMEN, Grace beseeches them:

                        GRACE
              Please, I beg you. Not our home.

Harrow, holding the baby, takes one last cold look at the village, spurs his horse, and rides off. Behind him the Young Soldier, throws Grace a compassionate glance.

Anne, stoic, places her hand on Grace's shoulder.

                              ANNE
                    We will not win today. Don't give
                    them the satisfaction.

Dillon has broken free but cannot break the line of police
around the cottage. Grace stares at him. So many certainties
destroyed. She bows her head and begins to sob, as the
Delorey cottage is rammed, and collapses.

EXT. CAHIR. CHURCH MANSE - NIGHT

HARROW'S HORSE and a lone DRAGOON ESCORT wait outside the
building.

INT. CAHIR. MANSE - CONTINUOUS.

Simple, but comfortable. Harrow sits at the OAK TABLE. Father
Cleary sits opposite him.

                         FATHER CLEARY
                    I have prayed long and hard over
                    this, Colonel. But I realise that
                    in the interests of restoring peace
                    and order, I must do what I must.

He sighs, uncomfortable and distressed by recent events.

                              HARROW
                    Continue, Father.

                         FATHER CLEARY
                    If I do so, do I have your
                    guarantee that while the courts
                    adjudicate the evictions, those
                    that have no shelter may find it in
                    my church.

                              HARROW
                    I have already given that
                    guarantee, have I not.

Father Cleary nods, and calls out.

                         FATHER CLEARY
                    Mrs O'Donnell!

Mrs O'Donnell shuffles in unwillingly.

                         FATHER CLEARY (CONT'D)
                    Mrs O'Donnell. Will you tell
                    Colonel Harrow what you saw last
                    night, should I say who you saw,
                    running from the grounds of Cahir
                    House?

Harrow looks at her attentively.

EXT. RUINED VILLAGE - NIGHT

Little fires as some families crouch in the ruins of their homes, others shelter in roadside ditches or huddled under walls.

Angle: Fergal sits staring at something in the rubble. Dillon silently comes and sits next to him.

Fergal turns to him and then silently lifts a stained CLOTH from the mess of beams and thatch. Revealing the half buried body of his father.

          FERGAL
    I've not the heart to dig him out.
    Bastards...

Dillon puts an arm around his shoulders.

          FERGAL (CONT'D)
    Meagher's asking for volunteers.
    I'm minded to join him, Dillon.

          DILLON
    He's all mouth and fancy coats
    Fergal.

Fergal glances around.

          FERGAL
    He's gathering arms it is. Unloaded
    from Dutch boats and hidden at
    Creggan's Mill, Dillon. We have got
    to fight back?! Will you not join
    us? Ronan and some of the others...

He stops as the sound of marching feet and a ring of LANTERNS appears around the remains of the cottage. A voice rings out.

          POLICE INSPECTOR
    Dillon Culhane. You are under
    arrest! Give yourself up.

Fergal leaps up, yells at Dillon

          FERGAL
    Run man! They'll show no mercy!

He disappears into the night. Dillon leaps up, runs from the lights... and into the arms of another squad of POLICE.

He struggles, downs one policeman, then another. A rain of TRUNCHEONS put an end to his resistance.

EXT. CAHIR. DITCH OUTSIDE VILLAGE - CONTINUOUS.

Anne and Grace are holding Clodagh tight between them, trying to keep her warm. They exchange looks at the CLATTER of hooves above them.

POV: Between the squad of MOUNTED POLICE she sees Dillon trussed and bleeding, draped over a horse.

Grace leaps up.

>   GRACE
>   Dillon!

But the squad is already turning the corner of the road. Grace stands in the moonlight, her shoulders slump. A beat. She stares up at the moon, asking for strength.

>   GRACE (CONT'D)
>   Help me!

The wind soughs eerily. A cloud passes over the moon

As if in answer to her cry: the sound of a lone horse. She turns to see, Meagher, mounted on Juno who glows a ghostly white in the moonlight.

>   MEAGHER
>   Grace! Omigod, Grace!

He leaps off Juno and sweeps her up into his arms.

INT. TIPPERARY. BRITISH ARMY GARRISON. ROOM - DAY

A large TABLE is set for a meal for two. Table cloth and silverware, though that is laid at one place only. A HAM HOCK, A DECANTER of PORT and STILTON CHEESE complete the arrangements.

The door opens and TWO GUARDS bring Dillon into the room, leg and wrist MANACLES clanking. He is bruised and blood from a broken tooth stains his mouth. The guards sit Dillon in a chair about six feet from the sumptuous table.

Dillon can't avert his gaze from the mouth watering table.

A beat: The door opens again to admit Harrow. He sits at the table. He begins to slowly cut a slice of the ham.

>   HARROW
>   Hungry Mister Culhane?

Dillon says nothing but his hunger is unquenchable. Harrow smiles.

> HARROW (CONT'D)
> Excellent ham this. Are you proud of yourself? Inciting a riot. Arson. Hanging offences. I'm sure you understand.

Dillon warily nods.

> HARROW (CONT'D)
> Sure you're not hungry Culhane? You are free to join me and after enjoying a good meal, maybe even walking free. All charges dropped.

> DILLON
> What do you want from me?

> HARROW
> Thomas Francis Meagher.

Harrow watches Dillon's face carefully. Dillon can't hide his surprise, then nods warily again. Harrow chews.

> HARROW (CONT'D)
> Plenty here for two, Culhane. By the way the reward for information that leads to the arrest of Thomas Francis Meagher is set at two thousand pounds. A Godsend if you care to collect it.

Dillon, with an effort.

> DILLON
> I'm not for sale.

> HARROW
> Not a very imaginative position Mister Culhane. I have reason to believe that you have knowledge of a hidden cache of arms that he has buried.

> DILLON
> I have no knowledge of such a thing.

There is the sound of a drum roll from the courtyard outside. Harrow crosses to the window.

                    HARROW
          We have a friend of yours below.
          Perhaps after you have seen him and
          corroborated what he has told us
          you can enjoy a good meal and your
          reward.

He motions to the guards who hoist Dillon up and take him to
the window.

POV: In the courtyard a half naked man is tied to a table
lying on it's side. As the DRUMS roll, a CAT'o NINE TAILS
WHIP lashes his bare back, drawing blood and a groan of pain
and anguish. In agony the man turns his head and we see it is
Fergal.

The guards drag Dillon back to the table.

                    DILLON
          He's told you nothing or you
          bastards would not be whipping him.

Harrow nods appreciatively.

                    HARROW
          Where is Meagher's arms cache?

Dillon explodes.

                    DILLON
          Never! I will not betray my people.

                    HARROW
          Meagher is not your people. He is a
          rich dandy who has led you all into
          great danger now and in the end
          ignominious defeat. You want your
          future back, I offer you the key.

He turns to the guards.

                    HARROW (CONT'D)
          Take him away.

As Dillon leaves Harrow, listens to the drum rolls and the
cries of agony.

                    HARROW (CONT'D)
          Dammit!

He shakes his head in distaste and pours himself some port.

EXT. CAHIR. CHURCH AND TITHE BARN.

The graveyard and barn are crowded with evicted families. A few fires burn. A temporary SOUP KITCHEN operates. Father Cleary and Meagher exit the church into the porch.

> FATHER CLEARY
> For God's sake, Meagher, you are taking on the most powerful empire in the world. An appeal to fight, to unarmed, inexperienced people is akin to suicide! Your only hope is negotiation and compromise.

> MEAGHER
> And allow this country to stumble along indefinitely on its knees, you're saying?

> FATHER CLEARY
> Submission, Mister Meagher, requires courage also.

> MEAGHER
> No Father. No more. Freedom from England's domination or death. I am resolved.

Cleary shakes his head in frustration. Meagher says quietly:

> MEAGHER (CONT'D)
> Father if I commit to do no act that is dishonorable or hotheaded will you grant me absolution.

Cleary sighs.

> FATHER CLEARY
> In these times, I suppose that is the best I can expect.

Meagher kneels, and Cleary makes the sign of the cross.

> FATHER CLEARY (CONT'D)
> Ego te absolve in nomine Patris, at Filii et Spiritus Sancti.

ANGLE: Meagher crosses into the graveyard. Grace is waiting for him, she looks spiritually restored as she looks at him.

> GRACE
> Thomas.

He comes close to her.

MEAGHER
I can't stay Grace. I have much to
do, a price on my head... and maybe
a bleak future ahead.

She looks at him, determined.

GRACE
A future I want to share Thomas.
Will you have me as a volunteer?

MEAGHER
No, Grace. Because of me you have
seen too much death already.

GRACE
Because of you I have learnt hope,
Thomas. O'Connell has gone soft. We
rely on you, Thomas to put an end
to this.

MEAGHER
You have a family Grace.

GRACE
It may be my fate to die, or it may
be my fate to win a place in the
hearts of our people and ride by
your side into the streets of
Dublin, my ears ringing with the
cry "Liberator!" Either way I will
do it at your side.

Thomas looks at her, emotional with love and admiration.

MEAGHER
Go on then, Grace Delorey. Say
goodbye to your mother and sister,
while I stand here and pray with
all my heart that I can ensure this
will not be the last time you see
them.

She looks at him, her eyes sparkling.

INT. TIPPERARY. DUNGARVEN ARMY GARRISON. ROOM - NIGHT

Harrow watches as a hooded Dillon's head is dunked in A TUB of WATER. His feet kick and struggle, and when it seems that he must be drowned, they finally let him up, and take off the hood. He is close to death, but manages to shake his head, defiantly, as he sputters up water.

Harrow glowers, frustrated.

EXT. IRISH COAST. ANOTHER VILLAGE - DAY

Grace and Meagher unload more WEAPONS. They are passed from the ship into WAGONS where they are hidden under the straw.

A pretty GIRL leans over the side of the vessel. Meagher smiles at her. She smiles back.

Grace notices.

Meagher smiles and shrugs.

They go back to their task.

INT. CAHIR. TITHE BARN - NIGHT

Anne makes more Johnny Cakes for the other villagers, when the doors burst open again, and this time English SOLDIERS pour into the barn, led by Walsh. He nods at Anne and Clodagh, and the soldiers grab them.

Anne fights off the first, punching him right in the chin, and grabbing Clodagh in a protective hug. But they are overwhelmed and dragged out.

INT. TIPPERARY. DUNGARVEN ARMY GARRISON. ROOM - DAY

A bruised and battered Dillon, burn marks on his skin, lies slumped against the wall. The water dunking equipment sits under the window.

The door opens, to admit Harrow.

                    HARROW
     Good Morning Culhane? Ready for a
     new day?

Dillon just snarls at Harrow:

                    DILLON
     Fook You!

Harrow does not answer, but simply nods to the door. Clodagh, in tears, and a struggling Anne are dragged inside.

                    DILLON (CONT'D)
     My God! You despicable bastard.

                    HARROW
     I don't enjoy torturing women and
     children. But their sacrifice is
     small compared to the greater loss
     of life it will prevent. Wouldn't
     you agree?

                    ANNE
          Let my child go. I'll suffer twice
          for her.

But Harrow nods to the jailers, who approach Clodagh with the
WATER TUB, and put the HOOD over her despite her struggling.

                    ANNE (CONT'D)
          No, not my daughter! You savage!

The HOOD is tightened, Clodagh is dragged towards the tub. At
the last moment, Dillon yells:

                    DILLON
          Enough...enough! Stop! I'll tell
          you what you want to know!

                    HARROW
          (dripping sarcasm)
          Good man. I knew you'd come round
          eventually.

EXT. CLEARING CREGGAN'S MILL - NIGHT

Meagher directs the new volunteers in digging up the sacks of
weapons. Grace watches, holding a torch.

Then, out of the darkness, English SOLDIERS on horseback
charge. The volunteers scatter, and are clubbed down.
Meagher grabs Grace, and runs for the trees. A HORSEMAN
follows. Meagher grabs the torch, tosses it right at the
pursuing soldier. He screams, burnt, and Meagher and Grace
make it into the forest.

EXT. FOREST - NIGHT

Meagher and Grace run for their lives, past tree trunks.
The burnt horseman pursues, seeking revenge.

Meagher hears, and ducks them both behind a tall tree. He
scrabbles quickly up the trunk, to a low hanging branch.
The horseman rides by, and Meagher launches himself. He
knocks the horseman to the ground, winding him, and knocking
away his gun.

Grace springs forward, grabs the weapon, and covers the
fallen soldier.

                    MEAGHER
          Who told you where we were?

The man says nothing.

                    MEAGHER (CONT'D)
              Tell me, or I will show no mercy.

Using his bayonet, he cuts his cheek. The soldier relents

                    BURNT SOLDIER
              A prisoner in Dungarvan Garrison
              jail. One of yours. Cal, something.

Grace gasps.

Meagher binds the soldier's hands and feet behind him, then helps Grace onto the horse. They ride away into the darkness, leaving the soldier behind.

EXT. TIPPERARY. POTATO FIELDS - NIGHT

Meagher and Grace ride through an abandoned field, the decayed dry leaves scrapping against each other in the wind. Silent tears trickle down Grace's cheeks.

Ahead, an abandoned farmer's lean-to is silhouetted against the night sky. Meagher dismounts in front of it, and helps Grace down. He sees the tears on her face.

                    MEAGHER
              Grace, I'm so sorry. For once I
              don't have the right words...

                    GRACE
              Dillon? How could he?

He cups her hanging head in his hands, gently wiping away her tears with thumbs. He smiles kindly and lovingly at her.

                    MEAGHER
              We will fight on. This is not the
              end.

She nods. And with that, she kisses him, tentatively at first - affectionately, and then as he responds, more passionately. The knowledge of being so close to death is let loose in their embrace. Meagher leads her into the lean-to and they fall into each other's arms and make love.

DISSOLVE

EXT. CAHIR TITHE BARN - DAY

The barn is quiet and strangely deserted. One or two fires smoke still in the graveyard.

Grace and Meagher ride up to the door of the barn, and he helps her down. Then he dismounts, touches her hand tenderly, They look around warily. Meagher puts his fingers to his lips. He unholsters his CARBINE.

INT. CAHIR. TITHE BARN - CONTINUOUS

They stop at the threshold. The barn is empty.

          GRACE
    Mother? Clodagh?

Only the wind answers her call. Meagher puts his hand on Grace's arm.

          MEAGHER
    If anybody is here, show yourself.

Silence. They exchange worried looks. A sound swings them around, Meagher's carbine points at:

Mrs O'Donnell, father Cleary's housekeeper.

          GRACE
    Mrs O'Donnell. Where is everyone?

Mrs O'Donnell looks around anxiously then beckons them to follow her.

          MEAGHER
    Best wait here, Grace...

She shakes her head. Mrs O'Donnell stops, beckons again.

          MRS O'DONNELL
    Come.

Meagher purses his lips. He gives Grace the carbine.

          MEAGHER
    I'll go ahead. Cover me.

EXT. CAHIR. THE MANSE - DAY

Cautiously they follow Mrs O'Donnell across the Yard. A DRAGOON horse is tied up by the door - Harrow's black stallion. Grace and Meagher exchange worried looks. A figure peers out of the window, then disappears. The door opens to reveal Father Cleary, who anxiously beckons them in.

          FATHER CLEARY
    Heaven be praised!

INT. CAHIR. MANSE. CORRIDOR AND KITCHEN - DAY

Cleary leads Grace and Meagher into the kitchen.

> FATHER CLEARY
> The soldiers came two days ago.
> They cleared everyone out, despite
> their promises, God have mercy on
> them. They took your mother and
> Clodagh with them.

Thatcher the Young British Soldier sits at the table. He gets up nervously as they enter.

> FATHER CLEARY (CONT'D)
> This good hearted young man came
> with news of them. This is Grace
> Delorey. It's her Mam and sister
> were taken...

> THATCHER
> I know. I've seen them about the
> village.

> GRACE
> Are they safe?

> THATCHER
> Yes. They are to be taken to Dublin
> tomorrow.

> GRACE
> What? What for?

Meagher gestures her to be quiet. Thatcher proceeds nervously.

> THATCHER
> Colonel Harrow wanted information.
> They were brought in to get it.

> MEAGHER
> What information could they have
> had, for God's sake?

> THATCHER
> Not from them. From him. The man
> they were torturing. He held out
> like a lion. Kept mum in spite of
> the floggings and drownings.

> GRACE
> What man?

> THATCHER
> He only gave in to protect them
> from what he had suffered.

> GRACE
> What man? What was his name?

> THATCHER
> His house was destroyed at the end
> of the lane there.

Grace's hand flies to her face, she knows the answer and it makes her sick to her soul.

> GRACE
> Dillon! Was that his name?

> FATHER CLEARY
> It was he Grace. Dillon. And I have
> to say a purer braver heart never
> existed. Thanks be to God he's
> alive still.

Grace's mind is reeling. The young soldier rises.

> THATCHER
> I must go. They think I'm
> exercising the Colonel's horse.
> I'll be hung if they find out the
> truth.

Cleary embraces him and shows him out. Grace sits down her head in her hands. Meagher watches her, shaken by her reaction, though for different reasons.

> GRACE
> What have I done? Misjudged him!
> All my life I've misjudged him...
> Oh, my God!

Father Cleary has returned and hears these words. His heart goes out to Grace. He goes to her.

> GRACE (CONT'D)
> We are all children of our times
> Grace, come now...

He embraces her.

> FATHER CLEARY
> These times are tearing us apart,
> my dear child. Weighing us down
> with regrets.

He looks at Meagher, but he mean himself also.

                    FATHER CLEARY (CONT'D)
               Everyone of us...

He looks back at Grace.

                    FATHER CLEARY (CONT'D)
               All we can do is to act on the
               truth that's in each of our hearts,
               my child. That's all we have for
               sure, for it's there our better
               natures are to be found. God help
               us.

Meagher listens, profoundly moved by these words, and questioning the motivations of his own heart.

                    GRACE
               I must go to him... No that's
               wrong.

She looks at Meagher beseechingly.

                    GRACE (CONT'D)
               We have to rescue them. Will you
               help me, Thomas?

Meagher sighs inwardly his heart breaking as he knew it would one day. Better his than hers he thinks to himself. With an effort he says:

                    MEAGHER
               Yes, Grace I will.

                    GRACE
               Oh, Thomas!

Suddenly enthused, she leaps up tearfully and embraces him.

EXT. TIPPERARY. DUNGARVEN ARMY GARRISON - DAY

TWO CARTS and a small MOUNTED ESCORT of DRAGOONS. In the first cart are Anne and Clodagh, chained together. In the second cart A battered Dillon and a seriously ill Fergal.

ANGLE: Harrow watches from a window. He turns away satisfied.

EXT. TIPPERARY. BLACK BULL FORD. WOODS - DAY

The ford lies at the bottom of a steep hill. The road crests the hill then drops down through the trees to the open space of the waist deep ford.

Hidden in the trees are Grace, Meagher, and O'Brien, plus some TWENTY MEN, some villagers we have seen, including Ronan.

                    O'BRIEN
Let's hope they're coming I have one hell of cramp in my leg.

                    MEAGHER
Don't tell me it was a champagne picnic you thought you were coming on, O'Brien?

Grace chuckles.

                    GRACE
And you two schoolboys are to lead an insurrection, God help us...

A low whistle distracts her. A boy calls from the trees.

                    BOY ONE
They have a scout ahead of them!

POV: A BRITISH DRAGOON crests the hill.

                    MEAGHER
They won't descend to the ford unless they get the all clear from him.

They concentrate aware of the danger.

                    GRACE
If I distract him, we can get his uniform. At a distance they'll never know.

Meagher considers.

                    MEAGHER
Let's get to it then. Liam, Robert and I will jump him.

Grace rises and darts to the ford.

EXT. TIPPERARY. BLACK BULL FORD - DAY

CU: Grace's shapely leg being washed in the crystal clear water of the ford.

The Dragoon stops, compelled by the sight. Grace turns and looks at him. It's THATCHER.

                        GRACE
            God! It's you.

Divining her intention he looks back over his shoulder.

                        THATCHER
            They'll be over the hill directly.

                        GRACE
            Will you help us?

                        THATCHER
            They'll hang me if they find out!

                        GRACE
            Then forgive me, but needs must.

She gestures at Meagher. Meagher and the others leap at the
soldier and pull him from his horse.

                        GRACE (CONT'D)
            Don't overdo it, Jesus! But make
            it look convincing...

They do.

EXT. TIPPERARY. BLACK BULL FORD - LATER

The two carts crest the hill. The escort stops them while
they scour the landscape. From the ford they see what they
think is the scout wave them on. They move down the sloping
road.

EXT. TIPPERARY. BLACK BULL FORD - DAY

Using REEDS, FIVE MEN submerge under the water.

From the trees Grace, Meagher and the others watch the carts
enter the deep water.

Concealed on the bank O'Brien cuts the cord holding a HUGE
TREE BRANCH against the current. The current takes it and it
swings across the path of the crossing horses. They rear up.
The escort cluster round.

Meagher appears and fires a SHOT. As he does so, the
submerged men emerge from the water and pull the startled
Dragoons from their horses. The second cart cannons into the
first, in a tangle of struggling horses and men.

Grace plunges into the water, and clambers onto the first
cart. Anne and Clodagh stare at her in astonishment as she
clubs their confused GUARD.

ANGLE: Meagher pulls himself onto the second cart. Men overpower the SECOND GUARD, Meagher lifts Dillon up and he and Fergal are lowered into the water.

As the men splash through the water carrying DILLON, others strip and bind the escort.

Grace, is hugging ANNE and Clodagh. She sees Dillon and giving her mother a hug crosses to him.

ANGLE: Dillon looks up into Grace's face. Tears spring into his eyes.

>   DILLON
>   Grace?

>   GRACE
>   Yes. It's me, Dillon.

>   DILLON
>   I'm not worthy of you Grace. I gave
>   away what I should have kept
>   secret.

>   GRACE
>   I love you Dillon, and I always
>   have.

>   DILLON
>   No. They broke me open... What did
>   you say?

>   GRACE
>   I said, I love you Dillon Culhane.
>   No more holding back...

>   DILLON
>   I'm feckin' dreaming...

And he blacks out.

INT. TIPPERARY. MANGER. SMALL FARM - DUSK

Dillon lies on a STRAW PALLIASSE. His eyes flicker open. He looks into Grace's face. He reaches for her. She grabs his hand.

>   GRACE
>   My God Dillon, they didn't leave
>   you any finger nails...

She kisses his injured hand.

                    DILLON
          They injured my body only Grace.
          Not my soul.

                    GRACE
          I'm going to make the world right
          for you, Dillon, I am. We'll be
          together, when this is over...

He squeezes her hand. She feels a rush of emotion.

                    GRACE (CONT'D)
          I am so sorry, Dillon.

Meagher has entered the manger, with a WOODEN BOWL OF BROTH.

                    DILLON
          Sorry, Grace?

His eyes stray to Meagher who having gently put the broth
down is leaving. Dillon understands.

                    DILLON (CONT'D)
          Ah. Well... He's a good man, Grace

She swallows. He squeezes her hand.

                    DILLON (CONT'D)
          Thomas!

Meagher stops and turns.

                    DILLON (CONT'D)
          Come here.

Meagher crosses to them.

                    DILLON (CONT'D)
          You both risked your lives for me.
          God help me, if I don't love you
          both!

He clasps their hands in his, they stand there a moment the
three of them, overcome. A holy family.

EXT. TIPPERARY. MANGER. SMALL FARM - DUSK

A few FIRES flicker. It's a small group of men. Meagher sits
alone on a low STONE WALL. After a moment Grace emerges from
the manger. She comes and sits next to Meagher.

                    GRACE
          He's not a better man than you
          Thomas, dearest. But he's where my
          heart is.

                    MEAGHER
          Nothing to explain, Grace. For my
          part I can only hope that one small
          part of that heart will stay mine.

Overcome he can't finish. Grace smiles at him.

                    GRACE
          Of course, Thomas. Yours for
          ever... and ever after.

Meagher looks at her his eyes full.

                    MEAGHER
          Then I'm a lucky man, Grace.
          Luckier than I deserve.

She squeezes his hand. A beat she stands before she goes back into the manger. Heart broken he watches her go.

                    DILLON
          Grace will you sing us the song you
          sang for us on the hillside.

She nods. And standing there in the evening light she sings.

                    GRACE
                  (singing)
          Alone, all alone, by the wave
          washed strand. All alone in the
          crowded hall...

Her song brings a stillness to conversations and movement of the miserable PEOPLE here, the HUNGRY ONES, the REBELS with their hope newly raised. It lifts to the sky.

INT. TIPPERARAY. MANGER - CONTINUOUS

Dillon listens entranced and feeling a burgeoning hope.

DISSOLVE:

EXT. WATERFORD DOCKS - DAY

Meagher, disguised as a blind beggar, stands with Grace on the dock before Anne and Clodagh, who are loaded up with blankets strapped to their backs and bags of belongings.

The ship before them is a stout, small two-masted schooner named The Virginius. It flies the STARS and STRIPES. They look up at the flag.

Very emotional, Grace hugs her mother and sister. Anne tries to put on a brave face, but she can't hold back her feelings.

She clings to Grace for a moment. Grace gently disengages herself with a final embrace.

Anne looks back one final time, then disappears into the ship.

Grace turns to Meagher, tears streaming down her face.

> GRACE (O.S.)
> (singing)
> But my heart is not there at all.
> It flies far away, by night and by day to the times and the joys that are gone...

The song continues over:

EXT. CAHIR. THE DESTROYED VILLAGE - DAY

Grace, waving the tricolour flag on a pole above them, leads a small troop of volunteers into her old village. Meagher, O'Brien, Dillon and Fergal are all near the front, on foot and leading horses. In the morning mist they make for a stirring, almost mystical sight.

Ragged villagers rise, incredulous, from the ruins. Father Cleary, handing out water to the survivors, also watches as the troop halts, and O'Brien and Meagher mount a cart to address the gathering emaciated crowd. After a beat Father Cleary shakes his head and disappears into his church and shuts the door.

DISSOLVE:

EXT. ATLANTIC OCEAN - DAY

A brutal storm batters the tiny Virginius. The huge waves come pounding down on the deck.

INT. THE VIRGINIUS COFFIN SHIP - DAY

Anne holds Clodagh tightly on the wet floor among hundreds of PASSENGERS packed tightly in the hold. People cough, vomit, some cry, others scream in fear of their lives. One WOMAN hugs a BODY which has been dead for some time. A CREW-MEMBER pulls the body out of her arms as she screams.

Anne turns Clodagh's face to hers, so she will not see the horrors around them. Anne takes up the same song as Grace, giving Clodagh comfort in this hellish place. As she sings she pictures Grace singing with her.

>   ANNE
>   (singing)
>   By night and by day I will ever,
>   ever pray, as darkly my life it
>   rolls on, to see our flag unrolled
>   and my true love unfold in the
>   valley near Slievenamon.

END SONG

INT. TIPPERARY. A SMALL FARMHOUSE - NIGHT

The FARMER shows O'Brien, Meagher, Dillon, and Fergal, both still weak but recovered, a map of the district.

>   FARMER
>   There is a coal mine here at
>   Ballingarry and the miners are on
>   our side. But then here, at
>   Mullinahone, is a police barracks.
>   A raid in force there will give you
>   many weapons!

O'Brien studies the map with dispassion but Meagher's eyes glitter. Grace looks at him smiling.

Prelap Meagher's voice and cheering crowd.

>   MEAGHER (O.C.)
>   We will only raise our people from
>   poverty by the blessing of an Irish
>   Parliament, that will nurture in
>   them a deep love of their country.
>   And I see over the dark hills of
>   the present a sun blest future and
>   a nation that embraces all...

EXT. TIPPERARY. BALLINGARRY TOWN. - DAY

Meagher surrounded by Grace, Dillon, O'Brien and Fergal addresses a small but enthusiastic crowd.

>   MEAGHER
>   People, of whatever nationality or
>   creed that come to make their home
>   in this ancient island.

He unfurls a FLAG Orange White and Green.

MEAGHER (CONT'D)
I trust that no one will refuse
this symbol of a new life.

EXT. TIPPERARY. ROAD AND FIELDS - DAY

The band of rebels, hopeful but still hungry march across the bleak countryside. Squalls of rain can't dampen their enthusiasm.

MEAGHER (VO)
And I trust that between its folds
the hands of all people of whatever
creed or colour may be clasped in
generous and heroic brotherhood.

DISSOLVE:

INT. LONDON. WHITEHALL - DAY

Sir Charles Trevelyan walks quickly towards his chambers. He is intercepted by John Abel Smith and Lionel De Rothschild, who last spoke to Trevelyan about a relief fund for Ireland. They look grave.

ABEL SMITH
Sir Charles, a moment of your time.

TREVELYAN
What is it, Smith? I am
consumed by crises today.

ROTHSCHILD
It is precisely the Irish crisis
that we wish to discuss.

ABEL SMITH
No doubt you have heard that my
colleague, O'Brien, and others of
the so-called Young Irelanders
movement are openly rising.

TREVELYAN
(impatient)
Yes, that is one of the crises of
the day.

ABEL SMITH
I beg you, negotiate. O'Brien is a
reasonable, peace-loving man. If
there is a way to avoid mass
bloodshed, it is your moral duty to
take it.

                    TREVELYAN
          A peaceful man does not openly bear
          arms against the government. It is
          he and Meagher who have chosen the
          path of violence.

                    ROTHSCHILD
          It is not too late, sir.

                    TREVELYAN
          If we let these traitors go
          free what will happen in India?
          In Africa? All across the British
          Empire? I will not be the one to
          cause the sun to set on our great
          nation. Good day sirs.

Trevelyan turns and hurries away. Abel Smith and Rothschild
share a troubled look. They turn and head off disconsolately
in the other direction.

EXT. CAHIR. THE EDGE OF THE VILLAGE - DAWN

The small band of rebels sit under Grace's Irish tricolour
before moving on. CAHIR HOUSE with its ruined west wing
stands bleakly above them on its hill. A few other MEN join
the group: one has a flintlock piece, another a pitchfork.
But there are few guns to be seen.

EXT. CAHIR. CAHIR HOUSE - DAY

The ruined west wing stands gauntly in the rising sun. A
yapping comes from within the precarious burnt out ruin.

Lady Mangan appears with a small PLATE OF FOOD. Enough to
give a starving villager a good meal.

                    LADY MANGAN
          Sinbad! Where are you, Sinbad?

She looks around, grimaces at the Tricolour flying in the
wind above the village below.

The yapping continues from the ruin. Lady Mangan approaches
it. She peers into the ruin. Down below, through the burnt
out floor there is a movement in the exposed cellar.

Nervously Lady Mangan tests the badly damaged floor that
leads to a charred staircase. A voice startles her.

                    MRS WALSH
          Don't go there your Ladyship! It's
          a death trap now.

Lady Mangan looks at her with an odd desperate smile.

>   LADY MANGAN
>   He needs me Mrs Walsh. He'll go to
>   no one else.

She steps on to the fragile floor. It shifts and dust tumbles and rises in small black plumes. Lady Mangan freezes.

>   MRS WALSH
>   Don't move your Ladyship! I'll run
>   for Mister Walsh!

She does. Lady Mangan peers into the depths below her. More yapping and then a little whine.

>   LADY MANGAN
>   Sinbad? Good Boy!

Another whine and a scrabbling. Somewhere below something falls. A whimper of pain from Sinbad

LOW ANGLE: High above us Lady Mangan peers down. Sinbad whimpers again.

>   LADY MANGAN (CONT'D)
>   Sinbad! My little darling, Mummy's
>   coming! It's all...

She takes a few paces forward over the creaking planks when the floor gives way. A precariously balanced beam gives way, and than the WALL above it. With a shriek and a cloud of dust the wall falls in - burying all below.

ANGLE: The Walsh's appear through the dust. They call out but the answer is silent.

Prelap singing:

DISSOLVE:

EXT. THE ROAD WESTWARD - DAY

Amongst the trudging group of rebels, Grace sings, and others join the chorus, of Oro se do Bheatha Bhaile (You Are Welcome Home). The tricolour flaps bravely, but their small numbers are dwarfed by the forest around them. The rebels come to a crude hut where the dead are heaped up outside, and a few other DYING MEN watch with sunken eyes.

>   MEAGHER
>   (covering his mouth)
>   Fever, God help them!

A dying man stands and observes the cavalcade with his fevered eyes. Meagher tosses a bag of food at his feet.

> MEAGHER (CONT'D)
> Nourishment, sir. And God save you all!

But as they pass, the rebels seem chastened by this terrible place. The mad-eyed man eerily extends a hand as if to delay them, but says nothing.

DISSOLVE:

EXT. TIPPERARY. ROAD TO FERRANRORY - DAY

The rain has stopped, shafts of sunlight streak the still stormy sky.

The rebels, for such they are, sit in small groups drinking soup. A small FIELD KITCHEN serving their needs.

Grace takes a pull at her soup grimaces in distaste.

> GRACE
> It seems not even Mr. Meagher can deliver us from nettle soup!

Grace laughs as do many others. O'Brien turns to Meagher.

> O'BRIEN
> We've precious few guns, Thomas for this endeavour.

> MEAGHER
> That's why we're going to get the police to give them to us.

> O'BRIEN
> Seems unlikely.

> MEAGHER
> Yes. We will first ask nicely and if they refuse we shall take them.

O'Brien shakes his head at his friends incorrigible optimism.

> MEAGHER (CONT'D)
> Why did you come, William? It is not a time to preach peace. There's no going back now.

> O'BRIEN
> I am not a warrior, Thomas. Though I know Ireland must be broken to be
> (MORE)

                    O'BRIEN (CONT'D)
          remade, I make no apologies for
          trying to limit the damage.

He shrugs ironically. Meagher puts a hand on his shoulder.

                    MEAGHER
          You are a good man, William O'Brien
          and I'm glad to call you my friend.

The pipers start to play a song of Irish nationalism
("RoddyMaCawley").

EXT. THE BARRICADE - DAY

The rebels stand in the rain behind the newly constructed
BARRICADE waiting for the inevitable attack.

A company of ARMED IRISH POLICE in blue uniforms suddenly
crests the hill ahead. The VILLAGERS and REBELS hoot and boo
and deride the police as they march forward.

The police halt some distance from the barricade. Meagher
silences the rebels, stands, addresses the police:

                    MEAGHER
          I am Thomas Francis Meagher, and
          this flag is the standard of the
          free Irish.
              (points to the tricolor flag)
          As Irishmen, it is your duty to
          join us. Lay down your arms, and
          you will be free to go.

The rebels laugh at his temerity, others jeer.

The police, confer amongst themselves. Then abruptly run up a
laneway towards a house on the crest of the hill.

Meagher waves his rebels forward. O'Brien, Fergal, and Dillon
lead the charge, firing at the police. Grace is amidst them
all, armed only with the precious banner.

The police make it to the safety of the house and fire back
from the windows. Two rebel men fall. Grace tumbles as:

The rebels take cover behind walls, trees, outhouses -
anything to shield them from the gunfire coming from the
house.

Dillon is suddenly at Grace's side.

                    GRACE
          I'm all right. Took a tumble is
          all.

She grabs the fallen flag and hoists it aloft, BULLETS tear into it.

Dillon smiles at her in relief and encouragement

ANGLE: Behind a small HAYSTACK in the garden, O'Brien and Meagher confer with Fergal and a group of rebels.

                    FERGAL
          This house belongs to a Widow
          McCormack. She's not at home, but
          there are five of her young
          children in there with the police.

Dillon arrives.

                    DILLON
          Grab some of that hay. Follow us to
          the door. If we get under their
          line of fire, we can smoke them
          out. Give us covering fire.

Meagher nods and does so as Dillon and Fergal lead the charge right into deadly fire. Two more rebels fall but others, including Fergal and Dillon, reach the door and begin to pile hay, which they set alight. But it only smokes, and the police inside fire down at them.

                    FERGAL
          Too wet!

Dillon signals the retreat, bullets whizzing all around. They bolt for the safety of the wall. Another YOUNG REBEL is hit in the leg, and falls.

Grace vaults over the wall, running to the fallen rebel. She helps him back to his feet as the gunfire intensifies. Fergal and Dillon reach her. Together, they carry the wounded man to safety behind the wall.

ANGLE: At the haystack with O'Brien and Meagher, a distraught MRS MCCORMACK, 35, arrives and appeals to them:

                    MRS MCCORMACK
          Please, my good sirs. My children
          are inside.

O'Brien gives Meagher a "this complicates things" look. Meagher makes a move to stand. O'Brien waves him back.

O'Brien goes to the gate and yells around it, waving a white handkerchief:

                    O'BRIEN
            A truce! The children's mother is
            here.

ANGLE: The house. The police fire sputters out. Faces appear
at the windows.

                    O'BRIEN (CONT'D)
            She would like to see to their
            safety!

ANGLE: From within the house comes a shout.

                    POLICE INSPECTOR
            Approach. Only four of you!

ANGLE: O'Brien beckons Mrs McCormack, and they stand. Fergal
and Dillon again volunteer. The four approach a main window
near the door. The police Inspector appears behind a window.

                    POLICE INSPECTOR (CONT'D)
            Mr. O'Brien, is it? And I believe
            Mr. Meagher is also here. Men too
            good to fire upon, but we are under
            orders.

                    O'BRIEN
            Why not give up your arms? There is
            no reason Irish should shoot Irish.

                    POLICE INSPECTOR
            We are Irishmen, yes, but men with
            families.

O'Brien beckons Mrs McCormack, they, Dillon and Fergal
approach a main window near the door. The Police Inspector reappears behind the side window.

                    POLICE INSPECTOR (CONT'D)
            Bring the children to the window!

The YOUNG MCCORMACKS emerge from the gloom of the interior
and one, around 5, appears at the window.

                    YOUNG MCCORMACK
            Are you coming inside, Ma? I'm not
            crying.

                    YOUNG MCCORMACK 2
            Matt's crying.

                    POLICE INSPECTOR
                        (to O'Brien)
              Some of the boys would love to
              shake your hand, sir.

He makes room for MEN behind him. Hands come out the window
for O'Brien to shake.

                    POLICEMAN 2
              Thank you for your years arguing in
              London, sir!

                    O'BRIEN
              Boys, We are your countrymen. If
              you will not come over to join us
              at least surrender your carbines...
              We need your help.

ANGLE: Inside the house a furious discussion begins amongst
the police. O'Brien encouraged turns to nod at Meagher.

                    MRS MCCORMACK
                        (to the chief policeman)
              Could I come in and join the little
              ones, sir?

The Inspector nods, and O'Brien helps Mrs McCormack climb
into the window.

ANGLE: A VILLAGE BOY gallops up on a horse.

                    BOY
              Soldiers are coming! Regiments of
              them!

ANGLE: Over the brow of the hill a line of RED COATED
DRAGOONS appear.

ANGLE: Grace fights the fear that rises within her.

ANGLE: Meagher can't hide his frustration.

                    MEAGHER
              Thank you, lad! Get home now and
              stay indoors. Friends, we must
              retreat to the town. The army is
              coming. Down to the barricades!

The rebels fall back, Grace amidst them all, still with her
flag. A voice calls from the house.

                    POLICE INSPECTOR
              Mr. O'Brien! We wish you well!

Police fire a few shots as they retreat, all aimed high.

EXT. TIPPERARY, FERRANRORY. BARRICADE - DAY

Dillon watches as Grace plants the pole with the Irish tricolour atop the barricade, then raises her pike defiantly. Her eyes meet Dillon's - they nod to one another.

The rebels cheer as Meagher and O'Brien walk to the front of the barricade. They all raise their pikes in tribute and rebellion - an awesome sight.

But then, a hush falls as the first DRAGOONS appear. TWO

COLUMNS, Major Harrow at their head.

Dillon, Fergal, and Grace watch, intensely as Harrow halts his men some fifty paces from the barricade.

> HARROW
> Mr. Meagher! If yourself and Mr. O'Brien would be kind enough to come with me, everyone else will be spared.

> GRACE
> We stand together. You will not separate us!

The crowd at the palisades agree, cheering her.

> MEAGHER
> We have been led here by chance and the force of famine. We will hold this ground.

> HARROW
> You are condemning yourself. And these hapless people.

> O'BRIEN
> You sir, are responsible! Your government has condemned them to death for the sake of a market!

Harrow salutes and retreats to confer with his STAFF and the police Commander from the house.

ANGLE: At the barricade, Meagher addresses the rebels:

> MEAGHER
> Friends! Those of you who wish to leave, do so now with our thanks and blessings. Those of you who
> (MORE)

                    MEAGHER (CONT'D)
          wish to stay, do so with my
          admiration. But Mr. O'Brien and I
          do not intend to surrender. Is it
          not so, Mr. O'Brien?

                    O'BRIEN
          You are precise, Meagher.

Grace leads a cheer from the crowd. It dies away but no one
leaves.

ANGLE: Harrow stares at the Police Inspector.

                    POLICE COMMANDER
          Sir, please consider letting
          it hold for a day. They'll
          disperse overnight.

                    HARROW
          But they will still be traitors in
          the morning, sir. No, take up your
          duties.

Harrow briskly turns and canters to his troops.

ANGLE: At the barricade, Meagher watches the first line
advance at a canter. He mounts his horse, as do O'Brien,
Fergal, Dillon, and some of the other young rebels.

Pipes and drums are played by the villagers: a ferocious
Celtic tune. In unison with many others, Meagher makes the
sign of the cross, then draws his pistol.

As the Dragoons surge towards the barricade sabres raised,
Meagher and the other mounted rebels charge the barricade
from within, clearing it, and then colliding head on with the
Dragoons.

Meagher smashes into Harrow, and is knocked off his horse.

Dillon charges right at another dragoon, knocking him off his
horse and onto the ground. They wrestle back and forth.

Harrow gets out his pistol and shoots at Meagher, who
stumbles back, blood flowing from his leg.

Dillon takes away the Hussar's sabre, and lunges it home,
killing the soldier.

Meagher charges Harrow again, and they fall and struggle
together. Blood continues to pour out of Meagher's wound.

> HARROW (CONT'D)
> So, you are a man of flesh and
> blood, Meagher.

> MEAGHER
> And a man of compassion - unlike
> you.

Fergal bashes his way to Meagher, knocks Harrow back, and forcefully drags Meagher back towards the barricade -- where

Grace and other villagers use their pikes to fend of the charging horses, which baulk at the jump and cannon into horses behind them.

> HARROW
> Dismount! Dismount! Form a line!

NCO's echo the call.

Grace sees Fergal fall from a shot and heedless of the danger, she leaps over the barricade and begins to drag him back. A fusillade of shots ricochet. Dillon reappears at her side and helps manhandle the wounded man over the barricade.

Meagher is taunting the dragoons, standing fearlessly on the barricade.

> MEAGHER
> Beating you back are we!

He ducks at another fusillade.

Grace and the Dillon lay Fergal down behind the barricade. Fergal has strength for one last smile.

> FERGAL
> Avenge me, Grace...

But those are his last words. Fergal dies in her arms. Dillon has rejoined Meagher and O'Brien.

> MEAGHER
> They can't take us directly.
> They'll tire of this come
> nightfall.

A fusillade of shots, coming from behind them. They turn to see that the police, all carrying guns, now advance from the rear of the barricades.

> O'BRIEN
> We are trapped. I'm afraid we're
> done for.

They each raise their weapons, back to back. Harrow and the Hussars close in from one side, the police from the other.

Then, the police open fire.

The bullets whizz right by Meagher and Dillon. Miraculously, neither of them are hit. They look at each other, amazed. The police fire again. Dragoons race for cover.

>   POLICE INSPECTOR
>   We are going to hell or heaven with
>   you, Mr. Meagher!
>
>   HARROW
>   The police have turned on us. Sound
>   the retreat.

A soldier takes out a bugle and sounds the retreat. The Dragoons turn, and regroup at their end of the street.

An exaltation seizes the remaining rebels, and a ferocious cheer rises from them and the police. Some swarm over the barricade.

Meagher falls because of his wound and Dillon stoops to help him up.

In a fury Harrow signals a heavy set Dragoon and the two bear down on Meagher and Dillon, sabres raised.

Grace sees and grabbing a pike she leaps over the barricade and like a fury charges at the Dragoon who tumbles off his horse, narrowly missing Dillon and Meagher.

Harrow reins in as his men stream past him.

Grace leaps up and clambers to the top of the barricade with the Tricolor. The rebels cheer. Grace gives a sudden wince of pain, staggers, but continues her climb. She reaches the top and waving the flag stands there, the symbol of victory.

Harrow, smoking carbine in his hand, grimaces in satisfaction then turns and canters to his retreating men.

All heads turn to look at Grace. A spot of RED appears just above her heart.

CU Grace's face.

SUDDEN SILENCE AND SLOW MOTION.

Cheering faces, Rebels seeming to dance in the joy of victory. A bugle sounds distorted and almost heavenly. Dillon is waving at Grace.

Meagher throws his arms in the air almost joyously. Is this victory? Then:

Behind him a wall of Dragoons appears - MOUNTED RESERVES.

The Tricolor Flag waves above Grace. The BUGLE sounds the advance.

SOUND AND MOTION RESUME WITH A JARRING CRASH.

The flag is not waving it is FALLING, as is Grace.

On a HILL to the right, both INFANTRY and CAVALRY appear in numbers the villagers and rebels cannot possibly deal with. Meagher slumps in despair. O'Brien quickly makes a decision and turns to shout to the rebels:

> O'BRIEN
> Flee while you can!

The Police Inspector agrees:

> POLICE INSPECTOR
> Flee boys! Swear you were never here!

The police and rebels begin to scatter.

> O'BRIEN
> Thomas, go! Dillon take him!

Dillon is looking around for Grace. He sees the fallen flag.

> DILLON
> Oh, God! Grace!

He runs towards her.

ANGLE: CU Grace, her eyes are glazing, but she struggles up, grabs at the TRICOLOR FLAG. Stumbles.

DISSOLVE:

All heads turn to look at her. A spot of RED has grown significantly larger just above her heart.

DISTORTED SOUND AND SLOW MOTION:

Dillon catches Grace as rebels flee in all directions, police peeling off UNIFORMS.

ANGLE: Harrow advances with his reinforcements, through a haze of smoke.

Meagher appears on JUNO, another HORSE in tow. Dillon lifts Grace onto it, mounting behind her. She clutches the flag to her, as they ride away.

Behind them the Dragoons surround O'Brien who holds out his white handkerchief.

NORMAL SOUND AND MOTION RESUMES.

MONTAGE: The two horses with the dying Grace, Dillon and the wounded Meagher, leave the village.

They cross a BRIDGE. Gallop through a FOREST. Disappear over the brow of the hill, the FLAG streaming out behind Dillon and Grace's horse.

DISSOLVE:

EXT. TIPPERARY. ROCK OF CASHEL. OAK TREE - DUSK

The beautiful castle dominates the skyline. The horses foam flecked stand under the stand of trees.

Grace lies on a hastily assembled bed of saddle blankets. The flag still in her now blood soaked hand.

Dillon feeds her water from a LEATHER FLASK. Meagher is trying to staunch the bleeding with a COMPRESS. The two men exchange a hopeless look. Grace's eyes flicker open.

> GRACE
> Thomas... Take the flag and set it up against the sun, I want to see the breeze catch it.

> MEAGHER
> Quiet now, Grace. Save your strength.

> GRACE
> Please Thomas. For once do as I ask...

She smiles through her pain. Fighting back tears, Meagher picks up the stained flag and limps across to the ridge. Dillon watches him go. A beat, then:

> GRACE (CONT'D)
> I haven't lived for nothing, have I Dillon? No one can say that, can they?

Dillon can barely speak.

                    DILLON
          No, Grace. No one can.

                    GRACE
          Lift my head Dillon. I want to see.

He does so as gently as he can.

                    GRACE (CONT'D)
          Look. Is that not a beautiful
          thing.

POV: Meagher plants the flag and it unfurls in a sudden
BREEZE.

Grace smiles, licks the blood from her lips, gazes at the
flag fluttering in the evening sun, Meagher standing next to
it, Cashel Castle, on its hill behind it,

                    GRACE (CONT'D)
          He lit a flame, Dillon. It won't go
          out, you know, once it's lit. Will
          it, that flame?

                    DILLON
          No, darling it won't go out.

                    GRACE
          Good.

A beat: a smile spreads across her face.

                    GRACE (CONT'D)
          Will you marry me then, Dillon,
          when we meet again?

The tears sheet down his face. He struggles to speak. He
squeezes her hand, raises it to his lips and kisses it.

                    DILLON
          Of course... of course I will.

                    GRACE
          Can't ask for more then, can I?
          Look after him, Dillon.

To his despair, her eyes close for the last time.

We see what she has been looking at. The flag unfurled above
the beautiful country behind it. Meagher standing beside it.

The moment is shattered by the sound of a bugle. Cavalry, red
and silver glinting in the sun approach up the hill.

Dillon and Meagher exchange looks, eyes welling up. Meagher is heaving inside and struggling to hold in his despair and pain, as he knows this is Dillon's moment.

EXT. COUNTRYSIDE - DAY

Meagher and Dillon ride hard across the green fields. Many lengths behind, the squadron of cavalry, led by Harrow, pursues.

Meagher pulls ahead, looks back at Dillon. Shouts:

> MEAGHER
> Relax the reins. We need to save every ounce of our mounts' strength.

> DILLON
> I'm not the rider you are.

> MEAGHER
> Just stay with me, let your horse guide you.

They approach a fence. Meagher clears it easily, but his leg pains him greatly as he lands. Dillon hangs on for dear life, his horse jumps, and he almost falls right off.

The cavalry, disciplined, in tight formation, easily clear the fence and start to close the gap.

Dillon and Meagher ride madly towards some trees up ahead.

The Hussars are close enough to try a few pot shots.

Dillon and Meagher make it to the forest, their horses dodging trees left and right.

The Hussars spread out, follow into the woods.

EXT. EDGE OF WOODS - CONTINUOUS

Meagher emerges first from the wood. A stone wall is right in front of him. Meagher spurs his horse, who jumps over the wall, clearing it. This time, the pain in his leg is so severe, he almost falls.

Dillon is close behind, but his horse shies at the wall.

Meagher sees, and stops, turns:

> MEAGHER
> Come on! Turn, gallop, dig your heels in.

                    DILLON
          Go, go! Don't wait.

Meagher hesitates for another precious second, as Dillon
obeys. He gets his horse in position, and spurs it on. He
clears the wall, and is now in another field. Meagher is up
ahead.

The cavalry jump the wall cleanly, and are close upon Dillon
now. More shots are fired.

Dillon pulls his gun, looks over his shoulder. The Hussars
are gaining on him.

Meagher looks back too. He sees Dillon rein in his horse,
turn to face the Cavalry, and charge them.

                    DILLON (CONT'D)
          Ride, Thomas!

Dillon rides right at the Hussars. He fires, and one of them
is blown right out of his saddle.

Harrow, in the lead, fires, as do others. Dillon is hit.

Meagher thunders ahead, but looks back, to see Dillon go
down, hard.

Dillon rolls in the field, comes to a stop. He is face to
face with a young potato plant. He reaches out and touches
the healthy young plant, delicate purple flowers blooming all
over it. And then, his hand falls to the soil.

A Dragoon dismounts, rolls him over. Dillon is dead, a slight
smile frozen on his lips. His body is surrounded by blooming
potato plants; his soul is with Grace now.

ANGLE: Meagher, meanwhile, has gotten ahead again. He sees
another fence, with a road and a much larger forest beyond
it.

He rides as hard as he can.

But then, he sees movement on the road ahead. Another troop
of cavalry mass before him. He pulls up on the reins, and
turns, but Harrow and his Cavalry close in from behind.

Meagher looks for an escape, but every direction is closed
off by the English troops.

Harrow rides forward with two Dragoons:

                    HARROW
          Thomas Francis Meagher. You are
          under arrest for high treason.

Meagher nods wearily, pats his panting horse, and throws down
his weapon.

A Dragoon dismounts and shackles Meagher's hands, taking the
reins of his horse. He leads it beside Harrow's horse.

                    HARROW (CONT'D)
          It was all for nothing, you know.

                    MEAGHER
          Nothing? We fought a famine that
          has taken millions. Taken babies
          from their parents. Children who
          will never grow. Old ones, who
          should have died in their beds
          instead of a ditch.

                    HARROW
          You've helped no one. Some of those
          bodies in ditches were put there by
          you.

                    MEAGHER
          The sword of famine is less sparing
          than the bayonet of the solider

                    HARROW
          You are about to learn that is not
          the case.

Harrow, basking in his victory, leads them down the road.

EXT. THE MARKET, DUNGARVAN - DAY

Gallows on a platform. Stark and final.

Meagher, bound, and his military guards ride into the square.
The merchants and the people are gone and the place feels
deserted.

Meagher, a prisoner now, is bloodied, battered and wears torn
rags - a stark contrast to when he first rode into Grace's
village on his white steed.

A ragged, ELDERLY MAN emerges from the shadows. He sees
Meagher and stares. As the troop passes him, he begins to
slowly clap and croakily cheer.

OTHERS, hearing him, begin to emerge from laneways and shuttered buildings. They too take up the applause. More and more join them, until there are hundreds cheering.

To Harrow's annoyance, Meagher raises his shackled hands to them. A broad smile beams across Meagher's bloody face: a man battered but not defeated.

                  HARROW
        Bloody fools. They cheer for a
        failure.

                  MEAGHER
        They cheer because they had the
        courage to stand up. Yes, they fell
        back down, but they will try again.

PEOPLE are massing now, cheering and clapping, chanting Meagher's name. INFANTS are raised towards Meagher, as if he has the power to bless them.

Father Cleary is amongst them, now cheering himself.

Harrow and his prisoner arrive at the platform of the town gallows. Meagher is roughly manhandled up to the noose by the soldiers.

                  HARROW
        Any last words, Meagher?

Meagher puffs out his chest. His words are wilful:

                  MEAGHER
        People of Ireland, I now bid
        farewell to the country of my birth
        - of my passions - of my death;
        a country whose misfortunes have
        invoked my sympathies - whose
        factions I sought to quell - whose
        intelligence I prompted to a lofty
        aim - whose freedom has been my
        fatal dream.

The crowd cheers his words. Meagher nods to them, smiles. Harrow steps forward - he's had enough.

                  HARROW
        For the crime of treason, Thomas
        Francis Meagher you are sentenced
        to death by hanging.

The crowd, angry, jeers and boos. People are shaking fists.

Harrow looks to the other soldiers. He is about to signal to them, when a single shot rings out in the square.

The crowd falls silent, uneasy. The soldiers, level their guns at the crowd. Nobody moves.

A patch of bright red grows on Harrow's pale shirt. He sinks to his knees.

Meagher looks down at him.

> MEAGHER
> You have not defeated Ireland. We do not blame your country, we do not blame your people - we blame men like you and Trevelyan. And we will take our country back from you.

Harrow lunges at Meagher, but cannot reply as he collapses, clawing at Meagher's chest. Then he slides to the ground, a look of defeat in his eyes as his last breath leaves him.

The soldiers scan the crowd, wary of more shots.

We see, in the distance, the teenage Ronan running away from the square carrying a rifle - a future revolutionary.

Another officer steps up - it is Lieutenant Sinclair, who tried to stop the earlier food riot. He checks Harrow, who is dead. A soldier approaches him:

> SOLDIER
> Sir, should we execute the prisoner?

> SINCLAIR
> No, cut him down. We will not incite a riot today.
> (yells, to the crowd)
> Thomas Francis Meagher will have his day in court. I promise you that all due process shall be accorded to him. Now, return to your homes. Enough have died today.

Sinclair looks to Meagher, a beat between these two young men. Meagher nods to the crowd.

> MEAGHER
> My good people, go home now. We live to fight another day.

And with that, the rope is cut from Meagher's neck and he is led to the jail as the crowd disperses.

EXT. NEW YORK CITY HARBOUR - DAY

Anne and Clodagh lean on the railing of the Virginius, battered but still sailing. They smile at the miraculous sight of the growing city before them - their new home.

>   ANNE (V.O.)
> Before it ended, the Great Hunger
> killed over 1.5 million Irish
> people. Another 1.5 million escaped
> almost certain death by emigration.
> My Clodagh married a lawyer in New
> York, and became an activist, from
> afar, for Irish independence.

INT. THE FIGHTING COCKS INN - NIGHT

Walsh, very drunk, fights a bigger, stronger IRISHMAN. Walsh takes repeated blows to his head, and collapses.

>   ANNE (V.O.)
> Walsh, Lady Mangan's steward,
> remained in Ireland, but never
> found proper employment again. The
> stench of failure stuck to him.

EXT. MOUNTAINS OF MONTANA - DAY

A horse and rider are dwarfed by the sunset-dappled Rocky Mountains.

>   ANNE (V.O.)
> Due to the public outcry, both in
> Ireland and England, the death
> sentences of Thomas Francis Meagher
> and William Smith O'Brien were
> commuted, and they were exiled to
> Van Diemen's Land.

The rider is none other than Thomas Francis Meagher, older and wearing a moustache and the blue uniform of the Union Army.

>   ANNE (V.O.)
> Three years later, Meagher escaped
> to New York. We saw him speak
> there, before he became a famous
>   (MORE)

                    ANNE (V.O.) (CONT'D)
          Union General in the Civil War, and
          then the Governor of Montana.

EXT. DUBLIN - DAY

Anne's GRANDDAUGHTER, 62, stands amidst a jostling, cheering crowd in front of the Dublin Parliament.

                    ANNE (V.O.)
          My Clodagh had her own daughter.
          She baptised her Grace, of course.
          I believe this Grace will live to
          see Ireland gain its independence.

The Irish tricolour is raised over the Parliament building. Anne's granddaughter smiles as the crowd erupts in joy.

                    FADE TO BLACK.

Printed in Great Britain
by Amazon